ROSE BUDDIES

ROSE BUDDIES

Jamey LeVier

To order additional copies of this book, contact:
Xlibris Corporation
1-888-795-4274
www.Xlibris.com
Orders@Xlibris.com
40605

This book is dedicated to the following people:

James & Edna LeVier (parents)
Tammy Wetzel-LeVier (wife)
Matthew, Makaley and Chad LeVier (children)
Jackie LeVier-Jackson (sister)
Jill Ann LeVier-Kriebel (sister)
Daniel Kriebel (friend for life)
Craig Conforti (friend for life)
Mark Timblin (Grandfather, deceased, and for
the most part "Grump" in the book)
Bill and Caroll Timblin (cherished uncle and aunt)
Gerald R. "Jake" Peairs (trusted advisor)
Daniel LeVier (the first LeVier to arrive in Parker,
PA from France in the late 1700's)

**Many thanks to the following people for their editorial
support and encouragement:**

Emily Kasten
Mark Majors
Robyn Moulin
Angela Hamorsky
Greg Haas

Author's Preface

Rose Buddies was nestled inside my head for several years, and until I came across the National Novel Writing Month website (www.nanowrimo.org.), I would have never had the muse, energy and courage to finish it. It is by far the most exhausting thing I've ever done, but also the most gratifying.

This book is fiction. However, all attempts were made to capture the true essence of the time through characterization and dialogue. My grandfather took me to The Rose Bud many times when I was a child, and therefore most of the characters are loosely based on actual people. Most of them are no longer with us, and those that are will forgive any characterizations that have come out unintentionally negative. This story is, in due course, a representation of the spirit of the time as depicted by the characters, and not necessarily a representation of the American culture everywhere. It is set in a very small, white country town in 1972. The town and other places mentioned are real. (Pictures of some of these places can be found at the end of the book. Otherwise, the story's relationship with reality is blurred.)

This book contains strong language and suggestive content, and in a couple instances racial dialogue. In no way is it meant to offend anyone; however, it was essential to be true and honest to each character, for without this loyalty the story would be disingenuous to the time and place.

It would be beneficial for the reader to have insight into the culture of this time and place—Western Pennsylvania, in 1972. Most of the population was white Anglo-Saxon Protestants. My family settled there in the late 1700's. They were French Huguenots escaping persecution from the Catholic Church. They are still entrenched in Western PA, except for the few of us who have moved to "the big city."

Coal was the largest industry there until its decline in the early '70's. Farming was also a prevalent source of sustenance. Most people went to church on Sunday and some of those same people were at the bars on Saturday night. People earned what they had, and welfare was a social scorn, not an entitlement. This place was, and still is, defined by toughness and blue collar work ethic. Parents spanked their children, and other people's children if necessary. A spanking in school meant a spanking at home because the teacher knew the parents. Life was simple, honest and unpretentious.

This book was not written in the traditional sense of classic plot pattern which consists of the conflict, crisis, climax, and resolution. Nor does it have a protagonist. Each episode in the café contains some elements of these, but it was not necessary to weave plot and sub-plot throughout the story. All sections basically stand on their own merits. The dialogue is what really shapes each character on every page and is not a progressive shaping. I did not try to change the characters from beginning to end as standard storytelling would advise; and there was no need to do so because all of these episodes take place in a single month, and people are not predisposed to change significantly in such a short time. Nonetheless, it's entertaining in itself as the reader considers the context of the setting and the personality of each character. One may feel sorry for these folks, having what many might call mundane and ordinary lives, but they didn't know any better. It was life as they knew it and they made the best of it.

Enjoy.

Introductions

The Rose Bud sat on a one-acre parcel of land at the top of the main hill in the small town of Parker, Pennsylvania. Parker was once home to 20,000 inhabitants and established its city charter in the late 1800's, but since has reduced to 800 if you count the pets. It kept the city charter and is known around the world, well, around the county actually, as the smallest city in the United States. It even says so on the signs entering the town.

It sits on top of the Allegheny River valley that runs to Pittsburgh, where the confluence of it and the Monongahela form the Ohio River, which runs into the Mississippi, which runs into the Gulf of Mexico, where the water evaporates and makes its way back to Parker on a storm cloud, which rained on The Rose Bud cafe that sat on the very top of the Parker hill along Route 268. Nature, like life, is a vicious circle.

It was built in 1950 by a guy named Bud. His wife was Rose. So he called it The Rose Bud Restaurant. Actually, it was more like a small country cafe. It was hewn of cement block and was nothing fancy to look at. Inside was a main dining area with booths lining the walls and tables filling the center. Capacity was perhaps 40 if you counted the waitress and cook. There was a small window through which walk-up customers could get take-out and soft serve ice cream. The kitchen and bathroom were in the rear of the building. Bud sold the place in the 1960's to a lady named Cookie, who promptly replaced the tables with a pool table and a pinball machine, hoping to draw a younger crowd. There was no booze license available so the only drunken brawls that occurred were after 2:00 AM when the Snake Pit and Parker House closed and the pangs of hunger that accompany all drunkards at that time of day lured them in by the car-full. They'd hang out in the parking lot, waiting for Cookie to call their name to pick up an order. At least once a weekend some lunatic would take another's cheeseburger and all hell would break loose. Cookie wore herself out in only ten years and sold the place to

Sylvia, better known as Sill to her patrons. She remodeled the place and made sure it didn't stay open past 6:00 PM.

Sill was a single attractive Italian woman. She loved people and had a few inherited dollars to spend. She paid cash for The Rose Bud and gave it a facial. Like most cafes, the morning crowd was made up of a nucleus of men who loved food and talk before the sun got too high in the sky. They were a hodge-podge of grumpy old men, a preacher, retired professor, truck driver, the cold and warm hearted, assholes and bastards alike. This made for good conversation. The year was 1972.

There were two young and pretty waitresses on the morning shift. This kept half the men coming back every morning and the other half staying until noon for lunch. Sill was no dummy.

Jill was called Jill the Pill because, when dealing with the morning patrons, she didn't take shit from anyone and knew how to give it back. They loved her.

The other waitress was Betsy the Babe and lived up to this name by wearing revealing shirts and tight jeans. She'd often bend over to let the old boys have a look while she refilled their coffee, and on occasion if she wanted to give one a near heart attack, she'd lick her shiny lips and say "mmmmm, that looks so good" in her sexiest tone. The tips got bigger on those days. She was a Junior in high school and worked for Sill in the summer. Her goal in life was to either find a rich man to marry or become a cosmetologist (which she referred to as 'hair dresser' because she consistently forgot that 'big word').

Elmer, better known as Duck because when he talked it sounded like he was quacking, had the biggest hooked nose anyone had ever seen. It stopped children in their tracks. It was enough to make Cyrano de Bergerac jealous; in fact one of the men, Ray, wanted to call Elmer "CD," but thought better of it and just went with Duck. Elmer the Duck was a retired coal miner who had lost his wife shortly after retirement. She didn't die. He literally lost her. After retirement he convinced her to go with him on an Alaskan adventure tour. About mid-way into the short snowshoe hike, they got separated from their group and unbeknownst stumbled onto a frozen river. Mrs. Duck broke through the ice and was never found.

Elmer was devastated. He went back home and became a hermit for a few years. One day, out of the blue, his friend Mark called and convinced him to have breakfast at The Rose Bud; it was under new management and the lady was a looker. Elmer agreed.

Mark the Grump, Duck's long-time friend, was also retired and living on a small pension from the oil refinery and Social Security benefits. He raised eight children, and his wife of nearly fifty years was quite stern. The morning jaunts to The Rose Bud were his daily reprieve, and he was normally back by the time the stern one rolled out of bed. Every day was a scolding for going up there to that greasy spoon to look at the slutty waitresses. In Mark's opinion, it was worth it. But he was perpetually grumpy and Sill started calling him Grump. It stuck. One day for his birthday Sill brought out a present and laid it on the table in front of him. He opened it and smiled. It was a vanity license plate for the front of his car. It had the name "Grump" painted on it. From that day forward, he was known as Mark the Grump.

What they didn't know about Grump, and what he didn't talk about much, was his time served in WWII fighting Hitler's army. He fought Germans in hand-to-hand combat. He was trained to fight in close quarters by sticking the bayonet into the enemy's stomach, pulling the trigger and going to the next one. He'd wake up during bad storms; afraid he was under attack. There were many nights he'd get only a few hours of sleep. Add this to a stern wife and anyone would be grumpy. The only other person in the morning crowd at The Rose Bud who fought in WWII was Ed the Evangelist.

He was called Ed the Evangelist because he was an ordained minister. He never held a full time position at a church, but filled in when pastors went on vacation. He also did funerals and weddings. Ed fought in the Pacific theatre and was a naval officer on a battleship. One day near the island of Saipan his ship was hit by a Japanese torpedo. Fire bellowed up from the hull. He was on deck barking out orders and sounding the alarm. The ship started to sink. He went into the water with three hundred others. By the time the rescue squad arrived, the sharks had gotten all but forty of them. It was during this time that Ed vowed to God that he would become a minister of the Gospel if he survived. "And God held me to it," he'd say.

Being a part of the breakfast crew was his chance to be a solid witness to the heathens in these parts. If he were ashamed of Jesus, then Jesus would be ashamed of him. So it was a given that Ed would step into conversations and inject his religious views, just to prove to Jesus that he was a worthy candidate for the Kingdom of Heaven. And especially he loved to correct a guy named Paul, one of the morning crew and also known as Paul the Cold Hearted Bastard.

Paul owned a junkyard, a graveyard for cars, so to speak. He was so paranoid that people were ripping him off that he had several hundred cars crushed flat and stacked them ten-high around the perimeter of his property. He installed a steel gate at the entrance to the driveway, and he bought two Doberman Pincers and made them mean as hell. By day they'd stay tied up between the mobile home and big garage. By night he'd lock it all down and let the dogs run free without dinner. That way if someone would sneak onto the property the dogs could feast on a leg until the cops arrived.

Most of the community knew about the dogs; but there was one joker who always had to try his luck. This sly character was Tom; better known as Tom the Asshole.

One night he snuck into the junkyard by propping a ladder on a stack of cars in the lower section of the property. He climbed to the top, pulled the ladder up and then put it down on the other side and climbed down. His goal was not to steal anything, but to leave a note on the door of the garage so Paul would find it in the morning. He made some extra noise to attract the dogs. He heard them coming and they started to bark, getting louder and meaner by the stride. They got within fifty feet and he took the garbage bag that was slung over his shoulder and emptied the contents, then ran back to the ladder. Earlier that day he stopped along the road and gathered up the remains of a dead deer and put it in the garbage bag. It kept the dogs busy while he snuck around the junkyard to the garage and left the note.

Normally, Tom would steal something because he was known to do such things. He makes a living stealing and collecting workers' compensation insurance payments for a fake injury. He claimed to have gotten a debilitating back injury from a wreck while driving a company truck. He didn't steal that time because he only wanted to make Paul look silly. He stole several times from Paul and the thrill had waned. It was no secret that Tom was a thief, a liar and an asshole. But he wasn't afraid to show his face in public, walking with a cane and showing an occasional grimace for good measure. One of the public places he frequented was The Rose Bud for breakfast.

Most of the men at The Rose Bud could not stomach the sight of Tom, and that's why he sat in a corner two-seater booth next to the door—next to the door in case he needed to get a fast break, and in a two-seater booth because he didn't want to sit next to all the other assholes. No one would acknowledge his existence there, except maybe two others—one of which was Jim.

Jim was also known as Jim the Gentle Giant—a misnomer. He stood five feet eight inches tall and weighed one hundred seventy pounds. But he had the patience of Job and the strength of Paul Bunyan. And there was nobody he didn't like or couldn't get along with, including Tom the Asshole. The only other person that would even dare say hello to Tom, excluding Jill Pill and Betsy the Babe, and only because they had to, was Bobby.

Bobby was known as Bobby the Blowhard because he never shut up and he smoked like a chimney. He drove truck for a living and was called Blowhard on the CB radio. He was actually proud of it and even though he did not like Tom the Asshole, could not contain himself from at least saying hello to every person in the cafe upon entry. And since Tom sat next to the door, he was the first to hear it. Tom always sat there and Chuck was the only person that would sit with him.

Chuck was known as Cheesy Chuck. He was not very bright. He lived at home with his mother, a widow, and collected aluminum and glass to fund his daily trips to The Rose Bud. He lived across Route 268 in a doublewide mobile home; actually, it was two singlewides bolted together. They didn't bother to think about color scheme or aesthetics. One was red and white and the other was green. They called it their big Christmas tree. Their neighbor, on the other hand, lived in a well-maintained red brick ranch with a detached two-stall garage. His name was Ray. He was a retired Professor, so therefore everyone called him The Professor.

Ray would often stand in his yard and lecture Chuck, who sat on the makeshift front porch on metal chairs, having drinks with his mother. "You know," Ray would exclaim from the property line, "green tea is best. It's rich with antioxidants. Good for longevity and vibrant health!" Most of the time Chuck and his mom would shake their heads and pretend to understand and wave, and often murmur to each other "He's a damn nut." Ray was one of the first to arrive at the cafe in the morning. On his way he'd bang on the front corner of Chuck's mobile home to wake him for the day, "You're burning precious daylight, Chucky," he'd exclaim. And each time Chuck would greet him with a yell, "You're a goddamn nut!" Chuck and his mother were anomalies of the family. Most of their relatives had good paying jobs, except for Big Larry, not because he was lazy, but because he won the lottery.

Big Larry topped the scales at 400 pounds. He was a home improvement expert prior to his good fortune. He didn't do much of the work himself, but sure was the best at telling folks how to do this and what to do there. He hired high school and college boys mainly, on summer break, and they were happy to get paid. Their fathers were happy they were learning a craft that could so easily come in handy at home. One day Big Larry stopped by Whyte's Market and bought a Big 7 lottery ticket. He won but didn't tell anyone, especially not his wife, who was ready to divorce him for a younger, thinner man. He waited three months. His wife left him. He filed for divorce and she granted it. In Pennsylvania, there was no waiting or separation or cool-off period. When two people didn't want to be together anymore, well, the judge granted it if it was amicable. She didn't want anything from Larry and he didn't want anything from her. The younger man was a hotshot salesman from Erie and she thought she was getting a gold mine. Her gold mine was in Larry's wallet. He cashed the ticket for $1.2 million and still told no one. He kept the money with a large bank and investment firm in Pittsburgh, living off the interest. No flash, no brag, no reason to either. He was quite happy just living with small desires and simple needs. It didn't take much to make him content. When people asked why he quit the contracting business, he'd say "Well, my buddy from Vietnam died and left me a little money from his real estate business, because I saved his life during the Tet offensive." "Oh," they'd say, not realizing Larry had never been to Vietnam, in fact he'd never been in the military, despite the fact that he always wore camouflaged clothing.

June 1st, Tuesday—The F Bomb and The Lord's Name in Vain

After his first visit to The Rose Bud with Mark the Grump, Elmer the Duck was hooked. The pretty owner and waitresses, the camaraderie with the breakfast crew and the fact that it now gave him something to look forward to each day were what pleased him most.

He was there every morning, 5:00 AM sharp, sitting in his car, a beat up Mercury Marquis, listening to Jack Bogut on KDKA radio in Pittsburgh. Duck's favorite joke was when Jack mentioned that he can't say whiskey on the radio, and therefore he will never say whiskey again, but he said it every morning in this manner.

It was June 1st and Duck had been the first one to arrive every day for six months. Sill was on time at 6:00 AM to open up the cafe. But this day was a little different. This day she decided it was time to help Duck. She went around back and came in through the kitchen door and shut off the alarm, then let Duck in the front. As was customary for the past six months, he locked the door behind him and started the coffee. Sill went back to the kitchen to start the grill.

The coffee was half perked when Sill appeared from the kitchen, "Coffee smells great, Duck."

"Thanks. It's my special brew today."

"What'd you do, add salt?"

"Yep."

"They have no clue do they? You could add arsenic and they'd still drink it."

"Yep," Duck replied. He took a seat in the corner booth by the large window in the front of the cafe, where he sat alone most of the time—alone—something he'd become accustomed to for the past several years.

Sill tinkered around until the coffee was finished, poured Duck and she a cup, then went over to sit with him and chat before the others arrived.

"So, Duck, tell me something. You've been coming here for six months and like a clock you are here at 5:00 and stay until lunch is over. And then you even help with the dishes. Why do you like this place so much?"

"Oh, I don't know. When you find a place that doesn't mind it when you roll Cutty Pipe on the table after breakfast, and lets you smoke 'em too, and a place where you can bullshit until noon, well, that beats rolling cigarettes at home and talking to yourself all day."

Sill held up her cup like offering a toast, "Well, Duck, that's a good enough for me to keep the welcome mat out."

They bumped cups and took a drink. Sill reached into her grease-splattered apron and held something in her fist. "Duck, hold out your hand."

Duck, puzzled, held out his calloused palm. Sill held her fist over Duck's hand, opened it and dropped something.

"What's this, Sill?"

"Something you've earned."

"Earned?"

"Yeah, earned. Listen, Duck, that's a key to the back door. There's no reason for you to sit in your car for an hour waiting on me. You can listen to Jack Bogut in here on the kitchen radio."

Duck's eyes grew watery. "I'm not sure what to say."

"Just make sure you have the coffee ready for me when I get here—and no salt!"

"Sure thing! I don't know how to thank you."

Sill stood up and put her hand on Duck's shoulder, "There's a comfort in knowing that you are here every morning to escort me inside. That's thanks enough."

Duck got up and made another pot of coffee, no salt, then unlocked the door. He grabbed a broom and swept until the first patron arrived.

Ray the Retired Professor came in, 7:00 sharp. "Mornin' Duck. Sill. Mighty fine day ahead."

Duck often said nothing but "morning," to prevent Ray from launching into a diatribe about nothing. He went over to fix a cup of coffee for Ray, three creams, two sugars, who by now was chatting with Sill in the kitchen on the benefits of a big breakfast with Eggbeaters. Duck sat the cup of coffee at the table beside the coffee maker, near the entrance to the kitchen. Soon, those four chairs would be filled by three others; Grump, Ed the Evangelist and Jim the Gentle Giant.

Jill and Betsy reported to work around 7:30, just in time for Bobby the Blowhard to make an appearance, "What's up y'all!"

Chuck dragged himself out of bed and made his way over. His hair, as usual, looked like a bird had peeled out in it, like a race car. He took a shower once a week, whether he needed it or not. He sat in the two-seater booth (the one Tom the Asshole would occupy), just down from Duck. His back was turned to everyone. Duck couldn't resist, "Chucky, what time did your alarm clock go off this morning?"

Chuck yawned and turned around, "Huh?"

Bobby took a drag on his cigarette and chimed in, "He said, what time do stupid rednecks get up in the morning!"

Chuck scrunched his eyebrows, "What's it to you, blowhard truck driver?"

Bobby chuckled. Duck asked again, "I said, what time did your alarm clock go off this morning?"

By this time the girls had made their rounds with coffee and didn't bother to take orders because everyone got the same thing every morning.

Chuck said in agitation, "That fucker Ray pounded on my trailer at 7:00."

Just then the door opened and in walked Tom the Asshole. Bobby blew out a puff and said, "Speak of the devil and he shall arrive."

Tom gave the door a pull and it slammed behind him, "You talkin' 'bout me?"

"Yeah," Bobby said, "Chuck called Ray a fucker and it reminded me of you."

Tom flipped him the bird and sat down with Chuck, "They pickin' on you, Chuck?"

Chuck stretched and yawned, "Oh, it ain't nothin' out of the ordinary."

"God, you smell like a ten day old dish rag," Tom said to Chuck.

Chuck stuck his tongue out, licked his middle finger and said, "Sit on it and rotate, mother fucker!"

Sill stormed out of the kitchen waving a spatula, "What have I told you boys about dropping the F bomb in here. Knock it off!"

The door opened again and in walked Big Larry. "Did I just hear Sill yelling at somebody," he said in a deep booming voice.

"Yeah," Sill replied, "these guys are dropping the F bomb again and I'm tired of it."

"Don't worry Sill," Larry reassured, "I'll just sit on the next one who does it."

"Thanks," Sill said, as she patted Larry on the belly, turned and went back into the kitchen.

Grump started laughing, "Hey Sill, will you spank me with that spatula if I drop an F bomb?"

Sill yelled from the kitchen, "I spank hard, Grump!"

"That's what I was hoping."

They all chuckled.

Jill and Betsy hustled the orders out, refilled coffees, then sat in a remote booth to enjoy a bit of peace before other patrons wandered in.

Grump had toast with peanut butter. "Hey Jill, come here."

"What Grump! I'm eating my breakfast."

"Come over here!"

"Damn it, Grump," she murmured, "What do you want?"

"This peanut butter is crunchy. You know I like smooth."

Sill yelled, "It's all we have Grump, unless you want to run down to Whyte's Market and get me some smooth."

Grump shook his head, disgusted, "Crunchy sticks between my dentures and gums and hurts like hell."

Jill shrugged her shoulders, "Do you want me to get you something else?"

"No," Grump answered, "I want smooth."

"Just scrape it off," Bobby exclaimed.

"Yeah," offered Chuck, "just scrape it off. That's what I'd do."

Grump snapped back, "Chucky, you just worry about scraping the dirt off your ass."

"Hey Grump!" Sill yelled from the kitchen, "Don't worry. I'll make you something special and I'll only charge you for the toast. Is that fair?"

"I suppose," Grump agreed.

Chuck could not keep his mouth shut, "Grump, you old fucker, just eat the damn crunchy."

"Chucky, OUT, NOW!" Sill demanded as she trotted from the kitchen.

"What?"

"OUT, that's O-U-T, NOW!"

"But I haven't finished eating."

"You don't have to pay," Sill responded, "Just get out."

Bobby was laughing and Tom said, "Don't worry Chucky, I'll eat your leftovers."

"Fuck you, Tom," Chuck replied.

Sill raised her spatula, "Chuck, I said no F bombs in here, now get out, now!"

Larry got up slowly and made his way over to Chuck's booth, "Chucky, you have two options here. First, you can leave peacefully and come back when you know how to behave; or I can throw you out right now."

"Take it easy, fat cuzz, I'm going."

As he walked out the door they all said in unison, "By Chucky!" and waved.

Chuck went to the window and flipped them the double bird. They all laughed. Tom ate Chuck's leftovers as promised.

As Sill made her way back to the kitchen, Grump said "Hey Sill. I'll eat the crunchy peanut butter."

"No Grump, I knew you had trouble with it and should have stocked up on smooth. I'll make you a cheese omelet."

"Can I have your toast, Grump?" Tom asked.

"No. I'll take it home and feed it to my dog."

A rare few minutes of silence settled in beneath the dim sizzling of Grump's omelet.

Ray broke the silence, "Hey, speaking of the F bomb, the versatility of that word has always intrigued me." A few of them rolled their eyes. Bobby offered, "Oh, no, here we go again," and lit another cigarette.

Ray continued, "It's an adjective, as in 'that F-ing jerk.' It's a verb, as in 'go F yourself.' It's a pronoun, as in 'you F-er.' And it's a noun, as in 'she's a good F.'"

Ed the Evangelist interrupted, "Ray, there's no reason to explain this. Let's talk about how the world revolves around the sun."

Jim the Gentle Giant agreed.

Grump was amused. "Go ahead, Ray, this is a democracy, and these two saps are outvoted."

"Wonderful," exclaimed Ray. "Well, where was I? Oh, yes, well, the etymology of such a versatile word can be complex. However, I once read several urban legends that postulated acronyms for its origin . . . ."

Ray was stalled briefly by Betsy, refilling his coffee, "Ray, what are you blabbing about now?"

Ray looked at her in disbelief that she had no clue what he was explaining.

Duck giggled and said, "Betsy, what'd you put in his coffee today, smart pills?"

Ray continued, "Some think the F bomb came from Irish law. When people were caught in adultery it was Found Under Carnal Knowledge. In England there were signs on the doors of people's houses that had permission to have intercourse that week, Fornication Under Consent of the King. Of course, these are just urban legends."

Bobby could contain himself no longer. He flipped open his Zippo and lit another smoke, "Ray, buddy, you forgot one."

Ray tilted his head at Bobby and lowered his eyebrows.

"Yeah," Bobby said, "let me explain it to you." He took a drag and blew it away, "the origin of the F bomb came from England, you're right about that. Back in those times, a bundle of sticks was called a," Bobby hesitated, looked toward the kitchen and whispered "a fuck." He paused and took another drag and flicked the ashes from his cigarette.

"Please continue," Ray requested.

"Well," said Bobby, "that bundle of sticks was, how do I say, a metaphor for a man's joy stick, if you know what I mean. And pretty soon, by golly, people were referring to sex as f-u-c-k. How it goes from there, I don't know."

"Very good, Bobby. That sounded somewhat educated," Ray said.

Bobby replied, "Yeah, we truckers ain't so stupid as you think, huh Ray?"

"Actually, I try never to have an intellectual dual with someone who is totally unarmed. But in your case, I'll let you off the hook this time."

Grump nudged Ray, "Get back to what you were saying."

"Oh, yes," Ray continued, "well, what I explained to you just before Bobby and I had our little chat was basically all urban legend. The real etymology of that word really comes from Middle German dialects of the 15th Century, namely 'fokken,' which means 'to thrust or copulate.' Other derivations are Norway's 'fukka' and Sweden's 'focka,' both of which mean the same as the Middle German."

Sill yelled from the kitchen, "Ray! Are you saying the F-bomb out there?"

Ray's eyes grew large. *It was just a lesson in the origin of the word.* Grump was snickering uncontrollably. Ed the Evangelist sat stoically and did not want to show any appearance of accepting such banter. Jim was listening intently, but had really never used the word much.

"That was pretty damn good, Ray," Bobby exclaimed, "I guess me and Ray are the only smart ones in here today."

Jill Pill came by Bobby's table and emptied his ashtray, "Ray's the smart one. You're the big mouth."

Bobby patted her on the ass, "I got something else that's big too, Jilly Pilly."

Jill pointed her finger at Bobby, "You touch me again and it won't be long."

"Long until what?" Bobby asked.

"I won't be long. Period. Get it, trucker boy?"

Duck laughed, "Good enough for ya, Bobby. You should know better."

"Sounds to me like Bobby just got his little stick snapped in two," Larry added.

Bobby flipped them the bird, stood up, threw down a five-dollar bill and said, "See you stick suckers later!" The door slammed behind him.

The Lord's Name In Vain

"Do you think he'll be back tomorrow?" Ed asked.

"I hope not," Jill answered.

Duck got up and made a fresh pot of coffee. Betsy was helping Sill bake the daily bread and Jill appeared to be shaken a bit from the pat on the ass.

"For your sake, Jill, I hope not too," said Ed.

"I'll throw him out if he does it again, Jill. There's no call for that. And let me know if Chucky does anything like that. I won't throw him out because he won't have the legs to walk in here with when I'm done with him," Larry offered.

"Thanks Big Larr," Jill said, "you're a sweety."

Grump got up and announced that he had to drain the main vein. On his way to the bathroom he stopped and pointed toward the booth where Tom had been sitting with Chuck, "Where the hell is Tom?"

Jim spoke up, "He snuck out when Ray was explaining fuck." Realizing what he said, he quickly held his hand against his mouth and muttered "sorry Sill" toward the kitchen.

"That dirty thieving bastard," Duck exclaimed, "Hey Sill, Tom did it again."

Sill walked out from the kitchen, her shirt spotted with flour, "Did that S.O.B. skip out again?"

"Yep," said Larry.

Sill shook her head. Larry quickly offered, "I'll take care of it Sill." He handed her a ten for his and Tom's breakfast and coffee, "Keep the change darling. I'll take it out of that bastard's hide."

"Thanks Larry. Jill's right, you are a sweetheart."

Larry blushed.

Grump came back from the bathroom and asked what the date was.

"It's June 1st," Duck said.

"Hey Ray," Grump asked, "what happened on June 1st?"

A collective sigh was heard.

"Well, Mr. Grump, let me tell you."

Grump chuckled.

"First of all," Ray said, "June 1st is the date on which most people get married. Also, in the year 193 A.D. the Roman Emperor Marcus Didius was assassinated in his palace. Those Romans, et tu Brute, my goodness, they were affixed with killing. Anyway, Kentucky and Tennessee became the 15th and 16th states in 1792 and 1796 respectively."

Betsy had been walking by on her way to the bathroom when Ray said this, and she asked, "Ray, didn't Columbus discover America in 1792?"

"Oh, sweetheart," he answered gently, "if by good fortune you get the opportunity to ascribe yourself to making a living with your higher than average physical talents, please do so."

"Ray," Betsy said, "if I didn't know any better I'd think you were flirting with me."

"It's all in the delivery, madam," said Ray.

Betsy winked at him and continued toward the bathroom.

"Go ahead, Ray, you were talking about Tennessee and June 1st," Grump reminded.

"Oh, yes, well, June 1st, let's see. In 1812, just 20 years after Columbus discovered America, according to Betsy" Ray chuckled, "was the war of 1812 when President James Madison and Congress declared war on England."

"I bet the English grabbed their sticks then," Duck offered.

"That's quite funny," Ray exclaimed with a chuckle.

Nobody else laughed.

"Let him tell the goddamn story," Grump exclaimed.

Ed grimaced, "Grump, do you pray a lot?"

"No. Why?"

"Well, you seem to say God's name a lot."

"What's it to you, Mr. Preacher man?"

"I don't appreciate you taking the Lord's name in vain."

"Oh," said Grump, "sorry." Then Grump looked at Duck and said, "Jesus Christ, if I knew he was going to get that goddamn offended I'd have kept my Holy Mary Mother Of God mouth shut."

Ed left.

Betsy saw him leave as she returned from the bathroom, "Grump, did you piss off Ed again?"

"He can't take a joke," said Grump, "He'll be back tomorrow."

"I have to go too," said Larry. "See you guys later."

Jim also got up, paid his bill, and when asked where he was going so soon, explained that he had to go change a tranny in a 1972 Oldsmobile.

Ray stood up and announced that he had to go mow his yard and do some reading before lunch. Then he'd check on Chucky to make sure he wasn't sore at Larry.

"Don't worry about Chucky," Grump said. "Don't get involved with family feuds. That's more dangerous than taking the Lord's name in vain."

"I suppose you're right," Ray said, paying his bill.

"Well, Grump, I guess it's just you and me," Duck said, yawning.

"No, Duck, I have to go catch hell from the wife for not coming home sooner."

"Sooner? It's only 9:00. Besides, you catch hell every day."

"See ya tomorrow, Duck."

"See ya, Grump."

"Bye Sill!"

"Bye Grump."

Sill refilled Duck's coffee. "Well, Duck, it's just you and me and the girls until the lunch crowd rolls in."

The door opened and a retirement age couple strolled in. Sill gave them a smile and the lady asked, "Just sit anywhere?"

"Sure," Sill responded, "Coffee?"

"Yes, black for me. He takes two creams and two sugars."

"Sure thing. The sugar's on the table. I'll bring you some fresh cream."

"Thank you."

The lady looked over and saw Duck sitting in the corner. He smiled at her and she returned it with a nod. Duck looked out the window, "Looks like it's going to be a nice day."

June 2nd, Wednesday—Camshaft, Harry the Hacker and Four

The whole gang was in full swing at the cafe by 8:00 AM, except Paul the Cold Hearted Bastard.

"Where's Paul been?" asked Duck.

"Who cares," spouted Tom.

"I do," Bobby said, "I need a new float for my carburetor. Unless, of course," looking at Tom, "you stole that too."

Tom flipped Bobby the bird.

"How original," Bobby said, holding a lit cigarette to his lips.

The door opened and Paul the Cold Hearted Bastard walked in and took a seat opposite Larry and Bobby in a booth near the bathroom entryway. Larry waved, "Howdy." Paul didn't bother to waive, but nodded his head. Paul was missing his index, middle and ring finger on his right hand. As a boy he helped his grandpa on the farm. He put the stock of corn into the chopper and it caught his glove. He's been sensitive about it ever since.

Jill came over and poured Paul a fresh cup of coffee, "Are you having the usual for breakfast?" Paul grunted and shook his head in approval. He was wearing a faded red t-shirt stained with motor oil and his belly protruded and touched the table. He was unshaven and wore steel-toed work boots that looked like someone had deliberately sliced the soles with razor blades.

Grump whispered across the table to Jim, "Watch this."

"Hey Tom?"

Tom would not look up.

"Hey Tom? I need a camshaft for my Torino. You know where you can steal one for me?"

Tom kept his head down, eating his breakfast. "Nope."

"The hell you don't!" Paul yelled. "I catch you in my junk yard again and you're a dead man."

Tom looked over at Paul, "You can't prove a thing."

"That bastard has stolen from me twice in the last month. That road-kill you're feeding my dogs is making them sick."

Larry interrupted, "Paul doesn't have to prove anything, Tom. You're a damned thief and everyone knows it. In fact, you owe me for a breakfast. You snuck your ass out of here yesterday without paying."

"Bullshit! I left my money on the table. Chucky must have taken it."

"Bullshit my ass. When I kicked Chucky out of here you were still sitting there eating his food. I paid Sill for your breakfast, now you owe me."

"You got enough money to buy all of us in here. Wish I had a rich Vietnam buddy leave me some dough."

Ray, who liked everyone—except Tom, joined the conversation. "Actually, Tom, this is a matter of principle, not a matter of who has more money than whom. You skipped out and Larry paid your bill."

"Fuck you, old man."

Larry stood up. As did Paul. "It's okay, fellas." Ray assured.

"No," said Larry, "It's not okay."

"Let's take him outside," Paul offered.

Tom dropped his fork on the table, eyes wide open at the two behemoth men about to kick his ass. "Listen guys . . . ."

Larry's voice boomed through the cafe, "No more talking."

Paul pointed his good finger at Tom. "Out."

"Don't hurt him too badly boys," Grump said with a chuckle.

"Yeah," Duck said, "He might sue ya."

Jill went to the kitchen and informed Sill about what was happening. Sill came out. "Listen boys," Sill said, "I'd like to see you beat the tar out of him just as much as the next person, but don't do it here. Please." She walked over to where Tom was sitting. "Listen, I can't stop these guys from taking you outside and giving you the whipping you deserve, so you best ski-daddle before that happens. And don't show your face in here again if Paul is here."

"This is a public place. I'll stay or go as I please."

Sill turned around, looked at Larry and nodded.

In a single motion Larry reached down with his huge right paw and grabbed Tom by the ear and twisted. Tom held onto Larry's wrist with both hands. Larry's movement seemed calculated and smooth. He clenched the back of Tom's shirt with his other hand and lifted. Tom threw a punch that landed square into Larry's stomach. No damage. Paul opened the door and

Larry drug Tom outside and threw him down. "You want more? Paul won't be as nice as me."

"Fuck you all, assholes!"

Paul made a move toward Tom. Tom jumped up and ran to his car, a beat-up Chevy Nova with dull magnesium wheels. He backed out and stopped on the road, revving the engine. It would backfire with every rev. He jammed it into first gear, applied the brake slightly and put the gas pedal to the floor. Smoke billowed from under the tire wells and formed a cloud that hung in the air. He let off the brake and continued to squeal the tires, laying a long patch of dark rubber on the road. Paul and Larry went back inside, laughing.

Chuck was finishing Tom's leftovers. Larry shut the door and glanced at Chuck, "You gonna pay for that?"

"Uhhh. Can you lend me a few dollars until tomorrow? Cuzz? Please?"

"You better get out there and pick up a few extra glass bottles and cash them in."

"I'm good for it, Larry."

"I beg to differ." Larry sat down. Bobby was firing up another smoke. Chuck begged, "Come on, good old cousin Larry, spot me for a day. I promise. I'll pay."

"Yeah, right," Bobby added.

Larry scolded, "You don't pay and I'll do to you what I just did to Tom—but much worse."

"I'll pay. I'll pay."

Larry handed him two dollars.

Chuck took the money and pulled a couple wrinkled dollars from his front pocket and paid the bill. "I'm going out right now to find glass, Larry."

"Sye-a-narra," Larry said with a half salute.

Betsy came by with the coffee pot and refilled Larry's cup. "Nice job, big guy."

"Thanks darlin'."

Jill brought out Paul's breakfast of eggs over easy and burnt toast. "Just the way you like it."

"Thanks, Jilly Pill. You burnt it good."

"That was Sill."

"Well, tell her thanks then."

"Actually, she said this one is on her. She appreciated you guys throwing Tom out of here." Jill turned around to Larry. "Sill said you're breakfast is on the house today too."

"Hey Sill," Larry yelled.

"Yeah?"

"You don't have to do that."

"That's okay. It was worth the entertainment."

Bobby couldn't resist, "Grump's the one that started it. Camshaft—my ass!"

Grump snickered, and then announced that the coffee was too damn strong.

Harry The Hacker

"Coffee tastes fine to me," Bobby said as he took a drag on his cigarette.

"Me too," Duck added.

"Here, put some sugar in it," Ray offered.

Grump covered the cup with his hand, "No, I don't want any sugar."

"Hey Grump," Betsy asked, "Did you get a hair cut?"

"No, I got them ALL cut."

A few of them chuckled at the old joke. "No, really, it looks nice," Betsy said.

Grump took a drink of the strong coffee, "Harry The Hacker did it."

"Who's that?" asked Betsy.

"You don't know who Harry The Hacker is?" Grump said.

"No."

"No, I guess you wouldn't. I'd like to see him cut your hair."

"He ain't touchin' my hair."

"Aw," Duck said, "He wouldn't hurt you."

Betsy shook her head and refilled Duck's coffee. "Then how did he get that name?"

"He cut off a kid's ear once," Bobby said.

"No he didn't." Betsy said.

"Actually," Ray offered, "That's an old tale he concocted for the first-timers. He kept a rubber ear in his drawer and pulled it out when a kid wouldn't sit still. He'd warn him that he'd cut off his ear if he didn't sit still."

"Ray, you could dry up a wet dream with the truth." Bobby said.

"You don't want to deceive this young lady, do you?"

"Hell yes!"

"Well, I don't believe in such behavior. It's better to just state the facts."

"Yeah!" Betsy said, looking at Bobby.

Bobby threw her a kiss with the hand that was holding his cigarette.

"I hope you die of cancer," Betsy said.

Sill heard it. "Betsy, get in here and help me bake the pies for today."

Betsy walked to the back in a huff. Sill went over to her. "Listen, you can't let him get to you. He's a jerk and a playboy, and you don't need to stoop to his level."

"I'd like to throw a hot pot of coffee in his face."

"Amen sister," Jill agreed.

"Girls. You'll run across a thousand Bobby's in your life, and every one of them will try to get into your pants in one way or another. That's all they want. Remember that and it will save you a lifetime of pain."

"Sorry Sill." Betsy said.

Sill gave her a hug. "It's okay, sweetheart. Just ignore him."

"I'd be glad to kick him in the nuts for you," Jill offered.

They chuckled.

Sill heard Grump yelling something about how hot it was in the cafe.

"Hey, Sill, turn the damn air conditioner on. Jesus, it's hot in here."

Sill walked to the thermometer. "Grump, it IS on. It's 70 in here."

"Feels like it's 90."

"Well," Sill said, "If you'd stop blowing so much hot air maybe you'd cool off."

They all laughed.

"Why don't you come back here, Grump, and work over the hot stove for a while."

"No thanks."

"She shut you up, didn't she Grump." Bobby said.

"Sill has a way of shutting everyone up when she wants to," Ed said.

"Who asked you, preacher man?" Grump said. "You gonna get up and leave today? I said 'Jesus' earlier. That offend you?"

"I left because I needed to take my wife to the doctor, not because I was offended. I didn't say anything because it was best just to leave."

"That was smart," Ray said.

"Ed can't be offended," Jim said. "I've seen you guys say things to him that would make me never come back. He keeps coming back."

"He's a glutton for punishment," Paul said. "Lord knows he's tried to convert me and I've dished out some harsh stuff."

"I'll get to you yet, Paul" Ed said.

"Maybe I don't want you to get to me."

"God knows your heart, Paul."

"Yeah, that's why they call me the Cold Hearted Bastard."

"Now, you know I don't believe that, Paul. There's good in everyone."

"Was there good in Judas?"

"Right to the point of his betrayal," Ed added.

"If you were raised to believe that that chair you are sitting on was a god, that's what you'd believe. I was never taught to believe in anything except my ability to survive. And that's what I do and that's what I'm happy with," Paul explained.

Bobby couldn't resist. "You're happy? If you're Happy, I'm Doc."

"Easy, Goldilocks," Paul said.

Ray laughed.

Jim whispered to Ed, "I don't think Paul knows his nursery rhymes very well."

Ed chuckled and whispered back, "I don't think he knows his classic children's stories either."

Larry stood up to leave.

"Where are you going so soon?" asked Duck.

"I'm taking my niece Rapunzel down to see Harry The Hacker."

Four

Grump looked at Duck and winked, then nudged Ray. "Hey, Ray, tell me about your pie again."

"Okay, Mark, but let me visit the restroom first."

Ray went to the bathroom and Duck said, "Grump, don't get him started again. It's enough to make me fall asleep."

"Yeah, Grump, why do you do that?" Bobby asked as he lit another cigarette.

Grump giggled and didn't respond.

They heard the toilet flush and Ray came back to his seat. "Now, about pie, Mark. It's actually P.I.E.S. It stands for the four elements of human existence."

"Oh brother," Duck said.

Grump was still giggling.

"But before we get into P.I.E.S., we need to discuss the number four."

"Why?" asked Jim.

"Because four is the most significant number in the universe, and by my proving that you will more likely accept my theory of the four elements of self."

"Oh." Jim said as he looked at this watch. It was 8:30 AM. "This going to take long, Ray? I have spark plugs to change."

"Uh, actually, what I'm about to say relates directly to automobiles."

"Really," said Jim. "I guess I'll stick around for a few minutes then."

"Good. Well, where shall I start? Let's talk about stability. If you try to ride a unicycle, it's very difficult because there's only one point of contact with the ground. However, if you add another wheel to the equation, you get what?"

"A bicycle," Jim replied.

"Exactly. And it's easier to ride a bicycle than a unicycle. That's a given. And why?"

Nobody answered, not because they didn't know the answer, but because they did not want to take a chance of encouraging Professor Ray.

"Because there are two points making contact with the ground. You get the idea, I'm sure. So, let's move on to three wheels."

"Yeah," Bobby said, "my cousin has a three wheeler. He flips the damn thing all the time."

"Precisely my point," said Ray. Bobby was proud of himself. Ray continued. "Three wheels are more stable than two, so what then would be more stable than three?"

Ray waited for the answer, like he used to do with his students, but was unable to resist telling the answer, "Four, of course."

Bobby perked up like he just got a revelation, "Hey, they should make four-wheelers instead of three-wheelers." He paused to take a drag from his cigarette. "Naw, nobody would buy them anyway."

"Actually, Bobby, that's a wonderful idea. But nonetheless, four is the most stable because it represents a solid, stable plane. A single point in space is unstable, like the unicycle. Two points, like the bicycle, makes a line, which is more stable. Three points, however, make a true plane. But four points, like the four tires on a car, make a stable plane. That's why four is the most stable number in the universe."

"I thought you said it was the most significant." Ed said.

"Yes, it is, but I just established that it is the most stable also. That relates to the stability of my P.I.E.S theory."

"So, how is it significant?" continued Ed.

"Glad you asked."

"This shit's getting too deep for me." Bobby added. "My eighteen-wheeler can roll over any damn car any day."

"Ray, this is very interesting," Grump said.

"Grump!" shouted Duck.

"Please continue, Ray," said Grump, smiling at Duck.

"Let's see . . . where was I? Oh, yes, significance. Yes, the significance of the number four is astounding. Let me give you a few examples. There are four elements of the universe: air, water, fire, earth. Four directions: north, south, east, west. Four seasons: spring, winter, summer, autumn. Four temperaments of humans: sanguine, phlegmatic, choleric, melancholic."

Jim whispered to Ed, "What's this have to do with cars?"

Ed shrugged.

Ray was still talking, and by now had stood up like he was conducting an orchestra. "Four tastes: salty, sour, bitter, sweet. Four communication mediums: hear, read, speak, write. Four existential elements: mineral, vegetable, animal, human."

Paul got up and walked past Ray and into the kitchen. "Sill, do you have yesterday's paper and a pen?"

"Sure. Is Ray driving you crazy?"

"I'm already there."

"Here's yesterday's Butler Eagle."

"Thanks." He walked back to his booth and spread the paper out, ignoring Ray.

"Four gospels. Ed, can you name them please?"

"Matthew, Mark, Luke and John."

"Thank you."

"Do I get an 'A?'"

"Absolutely, Ed. Now, let's continue. Four-year presidential terms. Four beasts in the book of Revelations. Four chambers in the heart. Even yours Paul."

Paul looked up and grunted, shook his head and continued reading the paper.

Jim got up and walked over to Paul. "Hey, Paul, can I come over this afternoon and see if I can find another tranny for a 1965 Oldsmobile?"

"What about the one I sold you last week?"

"Yeah. Well. I put it in and it didn't work. I want to bring it back and get another one."

"You always do this shit, Jim!" Paul was so loud that Ray stopped talking. "There's always something wrong with everything I sell you. Last week it was a camshaft. It was a damn wiper blade motor the week before that. You little weasel!"

Jim stood there and calmly asked, "Are you done?"

The room was silent except for Sill and the girls milling around in the kitchen. Sill sensed something was awry. Ray had taken his seat. "What's going on out here, guys?"

"Well," Ray said, "I was explaining to these fine gentlemen the significance and stability of the number four and Paul started yelling. I don't know why, but I think Jim had something to do with it."

Paul got up and said calmly, "Jim, bring that damn tranny over and get another one. But that's it. If it doesn't work, you get no more returns." He took a five-dollar bill from his pocket and handed it to Sill, "Thanks for the paper." And walked out.

Sill looked down at the paper and saw something circled.

Jim saw her looking and bent down for a closer look.

Sill put her hand over her mouth in shock.

Jim took the paper, closed it, and asked Sill to please throw it away.

Bobby, unaware of what just took place beside him, snuffed out his cigarette and quickly lit another. His Zippo snapped shut and he laid it on the table. "Well, that was entertaining. Jim, what the hell did you say to that Cold Hearted Bastard?"

Sill snapped back, "Bobby, stop being such a self-centered twit."

Bobby took a drag on his cigarette and blew the smoke towards the ceiling.

"Bobby," Ray said, "Are you pregnant?"

Bobby looked puzzled, "What?"

"Sill called you a twit. A twit is a pregnant goldfish."

"You're losing it, old man."

Ray replied, "Do you guys want me to finish my lecture on four?"

"No!" they all said in unison.

June 3rd, Thursday—Duplicity

Duck arrived at his normal time, 5:00 AM. He made an extra-strong pot of coffee. He almost forgot—no salt for Sill. Something was dominating his thoughts. That newspaper. Why did Jim tell Sill to throw that paper away? He went into the kitchen and dug in the garbage can. He found it. He opened it and saw what was circled. He shook his head and placed it back into the garbage can.

8:00 AM.

"Sill, who made this coffee?" Grump asked.

"Duck," she yelled from the kitchen.

"Duck, this tastes like mud. What the hell did you do to it?"

"Oh, it's my secret recipe. I call it my 'ancient Ducky secret.'"

"Well, keep it a secret and don't make it again."

Duck snickered and poured himself another cup. "Mmmm," he said as he strolled past Grump's table.

"Duck, pour that stuff out. I told you no more salt!"

Grump turned around to Duck, "Ancient Ducky secret, eh?"

Duck laughed.

Jill came out and took the Ducky coffee to the back and poured it out. Sill went out to make sure everyone wanted breakfast. Jill was in the kitchen and saw the newspaper in the garbage. She took it out and found the place where Paul had circled. She tore it out and placed the paper back into the garbage. She folded the torn piece neatly and put it quickly into her back pocket.

Paul called Sill over to his booth and whispered, "What did you do with that newspaper yesterday?"

"Uh, I threw it away."

"Where?"

"In the kitchen."

"Is it still there?"

"Probably, I didn't empty the garbage last night."

"Can you get if for me?"

"Why?"

"I need it."

"I have yesterday's. It came right after you left."

"I need the one you let me read yesterday."

"Ok. Let me see if I can find it."

Sill went to the back and dug the paper from the garbage and took it to Paul.

"Here you go. It's got a few coffee grounds on it."

"Thanks, Sill. It's just that there's an article in it that I didn't finish yesterday and it was really interesting."

"Ok."

Jill yelled across the cafe, "Hey Paul, why do you want that old paper? I poured coffee grounds on it this morning. Here, take this one." She started to take yesterday's paper to Paul.

"That's okay, Jill. Just mind your own business, dear."

"What the hell is sticking in YOUR ass this morning, Paul?" asked Bobby.

Paul was silent, concentrating on the paper.

Jill came over to refill Paul's coffee.

"Hey buddy. Need more cream?"

Paul did not acknowledge her.

"Let me take that paper and clean the grounds off of it for you."

She reached for the paper and Paul slapped his hand on it, "No. Go do your job and leave me alone."

"I guess he's got a camshaft up his ass," Bobby taunted, and took a drag from his cigarette.

Paul was frantically looking through the pages. *It was torn out. Did he tear it out right before he left yesterday? No. Is this the same paper? Yes. Somebody knows.* He tapped his spoon on his empty coffee cup. "Jill . . . refill."

She said nothing and poured him a fresh cup. She noticed that he had that section open and knew he must have seen where she tore out what he circled. His face was red and his hands were shaking. "Are you okay, Paul?"

"Uh, yeah."

Sill came out, "Paul, you done with that paper? I'm taking the garbage out."

Paul snapped at her, "Why do you want to throw it away so badly? Is there something in here you don't want me to see?"

As Jill stood there with the coffee pot in her hand, Bobby reached over and pulled what looked like to him a piece of newspaper from her back pocket. "What's this, Jilly?"

Jill turned around quickly, "Bobby give that back or I'll douse you with this hot coffee."

Bobby proceeded to unfold the piece of paper. Paul could see that it was the same shape as the piece from his paper. Jill reached for it but Bobby pulled away. "Well, what do we have here? Something circled." He held it as far away as he could but was not able to read it. "Damn, I didn't bring my glasses." Jill was able to snatch it from his hands.

"Jill, what is that?" Sill asked.

"Nothing," as she refolded it and put it in her front pocket.

By now, Sill put two and two together and realized what Jill had done.

"Jill, come back to the kitchen with me," Sill demanded.

The cafe was silent. A muffled argument could be heard in the back of the kitchen.

Betsy came out from the kitchen and asked who wanted refills. She was met with a choruses of "shhhhh."

Paul took his paper, left a five, and walked out to the kitchen. There were three muffled voices now, and very hard to decipher.

Ray announced as he looked out the window past Duck, "Why there's our good buddy Chucky!"

"Where?" Larry asked.

Grump scolded, "Shut up. Shut up."

"Oh," said Ray, "well, you can't hear what they're saying anyway. And it's none of your business."

"He's right," said Duck.

"Sounds like Sill's giving someone hell." Bobby said.

"There goes Paul," Ray said, pointing out the window. "He slipped out the back door."

Paul got into his tow-truck with Jill's folded piece of paper in his hand.

Larry excused himself and left. He walked across the street towards Chuck, who was sitting outside on the makeshift porch with his mother. They could see that Larry was talking to the mother and pointing at Chuck. Chuck's mom got up, went into the trailer for a few minutes, then re-appeared with an envelope and handed it to Larry. Chuck was furious. Larry opened the envelope and appeared to be counting money. Chuck ran into the trailer and slammed the door. Larry walked back across Route 268 and into the cafe.

"What was that all about," Bobby asked.

"Oh, I just settled up on a lifetime of debts with that little bastard."

"How are you related to him?" Ray asked.

"His mom and my mom are sisters."

"Oh. Where is his father?"

"He doesn't have one."

"Oh. Well. I guess that does make him a little bastard then." Jim chuckled.

"Paul sure pulled out of here in a hurry." Larry said.

"He forgot to feed his dogs," Jill said abruptly.

"He never feeds his dogs," Larry replied.

"Well, that's what he said."

"What were you guys talking about in the kitchen?" Grump asked.

"Nothing," Jill answered.

"Let it go Grump," Duck said. "It's none of your business."

"Yes," Jim added, "None of anyone's business."

"Both of you know something. What is it?" Grump asked.

"They are both experts at duplicity." Ray added.

"Duplicity, hell! They're hiding something." Bobby said.

Ray laughed.

June 4th, Friday—More Duplicity and The Wreck

6:00 AM.

"Good morning Duck."

"Mornin' Sill."

"Duck, can I confide in you about something? I just don't know what to do."

"Sure."

"Do you remember all the hullabaloo yesterday about that paper?"

"Uh, yes."

"I have a dilemma. Jill did something that I consider unethical and I just need to know if I'm overreacting to it."

"Ok."

"Sorry, Duck, I don't want to put you in a difficult position. I know you really like Jill. I just need an objective opinion."

"What did she do?"

"I can't tell you exactly what it was, but on Wednesday I gave a paper to Paul. When he got into it with Jim and left, he forgot to take the paper with him."

"It wasn't his paper."

"I know, but he circled something in it that was very personal and he should have at least taken that part of the paper."

"What did he circle?"

"I can't say, but it was very personal."

"Did he get arrested for drunk driving?"

"No. Please, Duck, that's not the point."

"Ok. Sorry. So, where does Jill come in?"

"She heard Jim telling me to throw away the paper on Wednesday. She came in Thursday morning and pulled it out and looked at it. She ripped out the part that Paul circled."

"Oh, I see."

"I'm so glad Bobby forgot his glasses or it would be all over the county by now. Anyway, when I saw the paper laying on Paul's table with that area torn out, then saw what Bobby was trying to read, I almost had a stroke. Poor Paul. Jill admitted to it and we swore to Paul that we would never say anything."

"What are you going to do?"

"Well, that's why I'm talking to you. What would you do?"

"That's a good question. Do you really think what Jill did was unethical?"

"Absolutely."

"Wow. I don't think it was."

"Really?"

"Yes."

"Why?"

"First of all, Sill, that newspaper was just garbage. You made it garbage when you threw it away."

"But she was snooping."

"Yes. But snooping is no crime. Have you ever eavesdropped?"

"Of course."

"Did you ever pick up the phone and listen on the party line?"

"Yes."

"Did you hear things that maybe you shouldn't have?"

"Yes, but they knew they were on a party line and that's the chance they took."

"Right. You knew there was a possibility that someone would see that paper if you threw it in the garbage and didn't empty it that night, didn't you?"

"I guess so."

"Jill is a good girl. We all make mistakes."

"Okay, Duck. I'm not happy about it, but I'll let her stay."

"Good. But just one more question."

"What's that?"

"Why did Jill tear it out?"

"She thought she was helping."

"Helping with what?"

"Duck, please, I can't say."

"Ok . . . well . . . anyway. Don't scold her for it. She's worth keeping around."

The Wreck

8:00 AM.

"Hey Chucky," Larry said, "You seen Tommy boy lately?"

"Yesterday." Chuck kept his head down, eating.

"Where?"

"Leave me alone, Larry. I'm trying to enjoy my breakfast."

"You gonna pay for that today? Don't expect me to bail you out again."

"Don't worry."

"Where'd you see Tom?"

"Why, do you want to go threaten him too?"

"Now come on, Chucky, I didn't threaten you."

"You told my mother you'd beat me until she couldn't recognize me."

"That wasn't a threat. It was a promise. Now tell me, where'd you see Tom yesterday?"

"I was fishin' in the Allegheny, across from the Parker House. I heard a car pull away, revving the engine and squealing tires. It was his Nova. Had to be Tom."

"You sure?"

"Looked like his. Why?"

"I heard he was in a bad car wreck yesterday."

Grump interrupted, "Yeah, he was. Heard it on the scanner and my neighbor is a fireman. Told me all about it. Somebody else was in the car with him too."

"Who," asked Larry.

"Danny Smith. I think." Said Grump.

"What happened?" Duck asked.

"Well," said Grump "I'm sure it'll be in the paper today, but they were drag racing across the bridge in Parker and the transmission locked up and threw them into one of the abutments."

"That's odd," said Jim, "What kind of car was it?"

"Probably a 1972 Oldsmobile!" yelled Bobby, as he started to laugh.

"Actually," Grump said, "Someone said it was a souped-up Olds 422."

"Yes. I put that tranny in," Jim said, shaking his head in disbelief.

"I'm sure glad Paul isn't here," Bobby said. "He'd have a fit."

"I hope they don't sue Paul," Jim said.

"Yeah," said Duck.

"They'll probably sue you too, Jim." Bobby assured.

"They shouldn't have been running it hard like that. They have no reason to sue me."

"Is Tommy okay?" asked Ed.

"Who cares!" said Bobby.

"You're quite the caring person, Bobby." Larry said sarcastically.

"Why, thank you sir." Bobby replied, and lit up a cigarette. "I take pride in my ability to care."

"Today is Tommy's birthday. Sure hope he doesn't die on his birthday." Chuck said.

"Actually," said Ray, "He would join the likes of Telly Savalas and Louis Armstrong, better known as Satchmo, for people who have died on their birthdays."

"Is there anything you don't know about?" Grump asked.

"Yes." Ray said.

"What's that?" asked Duck.

"Women."

"Women?" asked Grump. "You've been married to the same one for fifty years."

"Yes, and here's what I've learned. I've learned that they are unpredictable in their unpredictability. It seems as though I know everything, but my wife is always right. Can't figure that one out."

"Let's talk about women!" yelled Bobby. "I might be able to outdo old Ray."

"Let's talk about Tommy," Sill demanded. "Grump, are you sure he got hurt?"

"All I know is that both of them were taken to the hospital."

"I'm gonna call the Butler Hospital and see if he is there," Sill replied.

"Sill, what do you care? He's a bum." Bobby said.

"Bums," Ed responded, "are those that don't care about their fellow man."

"You callin' me a bum old man?"

Ed pointed his finger in the air like Ray lecturing, "A bum is as a bum does, son."

Sill turned and went back to the kitchen to use the phone, but Larry snuck in and beat her to it. She heard him speaking with the hospital. "Tommy. Probably Thomas.—Sill, what's Tommy's last name?"

Sill shrugged her shoulder.

"Excuse me ma'am?" Larry said. The lady on the phone described Tom's features. "Yes, that's him. How's he doing?"

Larry put his hand over the receiver and whispered to Sill, "He's there."

"I'm just a friend. Oh, I see. Oh, she is? I see. Ok." Larry hung up he phone.

"What'd they say, Larry?" Sill asked.

"They couldn't release any information to me because I'm not a relative. His mom is there with him."

"Oh. I hope he's alright." Sill said.

Larry walked back into the dining area and took his seat at the table with Bobby.

"Where were you?" Bobby asked.

"Called the hospital. Tommy's there."

"Is he hurt pretty bad?"

"I don't know. They wouldn't tell me anything."

"He's a gonner."

"Why do you say that?"

"I've been a trucker a long time, and I've seen my share of car accidents. If they were drag racing across that bridge and smacked an abutment, they can kiss their asses goodbye. A jolt like that will tear the insides of the strongest man apart."

Bobby had an unlit cigarette dangling from his lips and his hands were attempting to light it but his talking was interrupted the process. "And another thing, Larry. That kid had it coming to him. He's been nothing but a bad-ass thief his whole life. Always running from the law. God will get people like that sooner or later."

Larry squinted his eyes at Bobby, "Since when did you start believing in the providence of the Almighty?"

The cigarette in Bobby's mouth was now at rest. He clicked the Zippo open and a flame sparked up. Bobby sucked in a large drag and blew it to the ceiling. "It was cold. Eight inches of snow. Western Ohio is flat and the wind blows like a dust storm in the Mojave. I was hauling peat moss out to Defiance County and coming right back. I was young and stupid back then and thought I could take on the world. I never saw the car stop in front of me. I was a blizzard. I killed two kids that day. Almost gave up truckin', but it's all I know. I talk so much because I don't want to give my mind a chance to think about it. Why couldn't someone like Tommy have been in that car? Those kids didn't deserve to die like that. Maybe one of those kids would grow up to be President. All I can do to explain it is to say that it was God's will; however screwed up that sounds, it's all I got."

"How long ago was that?" Larry asked.

"Fifteen years today."

"That's a real shame, Bobby."

Sill told the others about Larry calling the hospital.

"Anyone want to take me up to the hospital?" Chuck asked.

"I will," said Larry.

Sill winked at Larry and shook her head in agreement, "You're probably the only soul in here that would help him out, Larry."

Just then Sill heard the phone ringing and went to the kitchen to answer it.

Jill grabbed the coffee pot and made a refill round.

Duck got up and went to the bathroom.

Sill returned to the dining area. "Chucky, the phone is for you. It's your mother."

"Aw, mommy's callin' again," Bobby mocked.

Chuck gave him a nudge and whispered "asshole" as he walked by. He stopped beside Larry, "Thanks Larry. Can we leave as soon as I get done talkin' to mom?"

"Sure," Larry said.

Duck returned from the bathroom. "Where'd the kid go?" pointing to Chuck's booth. "Larry, did you throw him out again?"

"No Duck. He's on the phone with his mom."

Bobby couldn't resist a dig, "Yep, he's a momma's boy. Makes you wonder what goes on in that trailer."

"Bobby," Jill said, "just for that, no refill for you."

"Aw, come on baby. I'd give YOU a refill any day."

"Bobby," Larry said, "behave now. Behave."

"Just messing around, Big Larry, I'd never hurt her."

"That's right," Jill said, "I don't imagine your tool is big enough to hurt anyone."

Chuck returned from the kitchen, walked past Larry and Bobby's table and went out the front door.

"I guess he's ready to go," Larry said. "Guess I'll have to pay for his breakfast again. Here you go, Jilly Pilly." Larry handed Jill enough money to cover his and Chuck's breakfast and a little extra for a tip.

"Thanks Big Larr," Jill said.

Larry winked at Jill and walked outside where Chuck was waiting.

"Well," Jill said, "I better go start the pies for today."

"Come to think of it," Ray said, "I never finished my story about PIES on Wednesday."

"And you can leave it that way," Duck said as he took out some Cutty Pipe and paper to roll it in.

"Duck, when did you start smoking?" Ed said.

"Since Ray started talking about those damn pies." And he promptly rolled the cigarette and borrowed Bobby's Zippo to light it.

"Watch him turn green," Grump said.

"You just sit there and behave yourself, Grump." Duck said. "I've been smoking Cutty Pipe for years; I just normally do it at home where nobody can see me."

"Ray," Grump said, "I'd sure like to hear about pies."

There was a collective sigh.

"Oh, most definitely. Well . . . P.I.E.S. It stands for the four elements of human existence; the Physical, Intellectual, Emotional and Spiritual self. I explained on Wednesday that the number four was the most significant and prevalent number in the universe, which supports my theory of the four elements. Now, let's see . . . the Physical You consists of your mass."

"Did you say 'blow it out your ass?'" Bobby yelled.

Ray ignored him and continued. "Your body is just molecules and cells working in harmony with all the others in the universe. The universe began as a clump of mass and it exploded. That was called The Big Bang."

"That's nonsense, Ray. That's what the evolutionists believe." Ed said.

"Actually Ed," Ray retorted, "The Big Bang fits nicely into the Biblical account of creation."

"How's that?"

"Well, the Bible says that God created ex-nihilo; which means 'out of nothing.' Do you follow me so far?"

"I think so. Go on," Ed said.

"Good. Now, the Bible also says that God created by verbal fiat; which means he spoke and it was . . . BANG!" Ray grabbed Ed's arm and startled him. "You get it?"

Ray laughed and asked again, "You get it, Ed? Make sense?"

"Yes," Ed replied, somewhat puzzled.

Duck, mesmerized by the conversation, had not yet taken a drag on his Cutty Pipe. It was lit and was half burnt away. The long ash had casually fallen into his coffee when Ray yelled 'bang.' Bobby saw it happen, so he got up and offered everyone a refill. "Duck, drink the rest of that cup and I'll refill it."

Duck downed it and didn't notice the ash. Bobby broke into an uncontrollable giggle and could barely refill Ducks cup without spilling it.

"Watch what the hell you're doing. You almost spilled that hot coffee in my lap. What the hell's wrong with you?" Duck scolded.

Bobby managed "nothing" as he turned and continued refills, still laughing.

"So," Ray continued, "God spoke and it was, The Big Bang. That's where all mass came from—nowhere, to now here. And that's where we came from. I'm not going to argue for or against evolution. I just wanted to show how our physical bodies came to be."

"Humans weren't alive back then Ray." Jim said.

"That's right," Ray said, "but the physical universe became a finite system. Mass is neither created nor destroyed, only transformed. The molecules that are in your body now were in The Big Bang."

"Oh," said Jim, adjusting his FORD, Fix Or Repair Daily hat, "that's interesting. You mean that tranny I replaced in that '65 Olds was in The Big Bang too?"

"Yep."

"Hmm. Interesting."

"So, now you know how our physical bodies came to be." Ray continued. "And this is just the tip of the iceberg. Einstein was actually the first scientist to prove that mass and energy were finite systems, neither created nor destroyed, just transformed, and he came up with the equation E equals M C squared, where E is energy, M is mass and C is the speed of light."

"Where the hell do you get this shit?" Bobby asked. "Everyone knows Einstein invented the atomic bomb."

"Yes, he did that too," Ray said, "but he also went a long way in discovering the properties of energy, mass and light."

Duck finished his cigarette and looked out the window. "Hey, Larry's out there giving Chucky a hug."

They all rushed to the windows to look. Chuck was crying. Larry put his hands on Chucks shoulders and said something. Then Chuck walked across Route 268 to his trailer. Larry turned to come back into the cafe and they scampered back to their seats. Larry walked in and sat down at his table, took a deep breath and a drink of coffee. Sill, Betsy and Jill were in the dining room, wondering what was up. The cafe was silent, except for the flick of Bobby's Zippo lighting a cigarette. "What's going on, Larry?" Bobby asked.

"Chucky's mom had bad news."

"Oh my God." Sill put her hand to her mouth and tears filled her eyes.

"Chucky's mom said she got a call from Tommy's aunt. Tommy died."

June 8th, Tuesday—Chicken

8:15 AM

Paul walked into the cafe. Everyone was there, except for Chuck. Jill was writing today's special on the board-baked chicken breast, mashed potatoes with gravy, carrots and a roll.

"Hi Paul," Larry greeted.

"Howdy," Paul said as he walked past Larry and Bobby's table and sat at his regular booth. Jill came over and poured him a cup of coffee. "I'll have your breakfast out ASAP Paul," Jill said and walked away.

"Jill," Paul said, "I need to talk to you."

"Okay. About what?"

"I think you know, sweetheart. Have a seat."

The coffee pot was shaking in her hand. "Mind if I get rid of this first?"

Paul waved her away. She put his order in and went back to the booth and sat down. "Well, what's up?"

"Jill, it's okay."

"What's okay?"

"The fact that you know that I filed bankruptcy."

"Sill?"

"Yeah. She called and told me that you ripped that bankruptcy announcement out of the paper to show your uncle."

"Paul, at first I was just being nosy. I heard Jim tell Sill to throw that paper away. I wondered what was in it that he didn't want anyone else to see. When I saw that announcement I was shocked at first, then I thought of my uncle. I just wanted him to know because he was always complaining about you owing him money for renting his crane."

"Yeah, I know. You were protecting family. I can't fault you for that."

"He said you are going to really stick it to him."

"I feel terrible about it, believe it or not," Paul said.

"It's none of my business. I shouldn't have snooped in the garbage. Curiosity got the best of me."

"I'm not allowed to talk to my creditors. Your uncle is one of them. Just tell him I'm gonna get on my feet and pay him. As for the banks, they can shove it up their asses."

"I'll tell him," Jill said; then went to check on Paul's breakfast.

Larry heard the conversation but kept it to himself. Bobby heard it also. "Don't worry Paul," Bobby whispered, "I filed twice and landed back on my feet both times. Hell, you'll have creditors kissing your ass again in no time."

Larry finished his breakfast. His elbows were propped on the table and his hands were folded as in prayer, "Sure feels a little lonely in here without those two characters," he said, looking at the empty two-seater booth by the door.

"Sure was a nice funeral," said Ray. "It's interesting how we view the dead. We're one of the only cultures that embalm our dead. Take Austria, for instance. I was on vacation there a few years back and we were driving around the countryside with some of our friends, and we came upon a funeral procession crossing the street. Everyone stopped their cars and turned off their engines. The priest was out front leading the entourage, and what looked like a younger priest behind him was waving the smoker, I don't recall the name of that thing, but it looked like fog coming out the top of an urn. And the pallbearers had the casket on their shoulders, carrying it with long poles. It was quite a sight. There was a brass instrument band behind them playing a dirge."

"Sill sent real pretty flowers," Ed said.

"Yep. You just never know when it's your time," said Grump.

"That you don't," Duck added.

"Ed," Betsy asked as she refilled his coffee, "do you think Tommy went to heaven?"

"Well, that's between him and God." Ed replied.

"Come on Ed," Grump said, "give us your honest opinion. We want to know."

"That is my honest opinion. I am no man's judge. God will judge."

Grump pointed his finger at Ed, "That's a cop out, Mr. Preacher. You're a big chicken."

"Grump," Jim said, "this isn't the time to get into this. A boy we knew was just buried yesterday. We don't feel like hearing this."

"Well, I do." Grump snapped.

"It's okay, Jim," Ed said, "I'll answer the question."

Ed took a drink of his coffee. "Well, Mr. Grump, let me ask you a question. You had a son that died at birth, right?"

"He was eight."

"Oh. Sorry. Well, do you think he went to heaven?"

"He didn't go anywhere."

"Do you mean he didn't have a soul?"

"When you die you die."

"Interesting. Well. Let's look at it this way. You believe what you want to believe, and I'll believe what I want to believe, and if you are right, neither of us loses. But if I'm right, Grump, you stand to lose plenty."

"Sounds like you are judging me," Grump said.

"No," Ed replied, "I'm not judging you. All I'm saying is that Jesus said if a man rejects Him, he will spend eternity in hell."

"Ok," Grump said, "if that's what you believe, then what about the American Indians?"

"What do you mean?"

"To reject someone, you first have to meet him. They never met Jesus, and they were very spiritual people, so do they go to heaven or hell?"

Ed scratched his chin for a moment. "God will judge the Indians on their own merits."

Grump asked, "Does anyone here know if Tommy was introduced to Jesus?"

Silence.

Duck shook his head and looked out the window. "Here comes Chuck," he said.

The door opened and Chuck walked in and sat at his booth by the door. Duck looked at Grump and held his finger to his lips as if to say 'shut up.'

"Hey Chucky," Larry greeted.

"Hi Larry."

Jill walked over and poured Chuck a cup of coffee. "You want breakfast today?"

"Naw, just coffee, thanks."

"How ya doin'?" Bobby asked.

Chuck shook his head, "Okay I guess."

"Listen, Chuck," Bobby said, "I know how you feel."

Chuck looked up from his coffee.

"I was in a bad wreck once and I killed two little kids. You just have to let it go."

Chuck stood up, "None a you guys liked Tommy. Especially you, Bobby. So don't pretend like you care. He was a good guy. Yeah, he stole stuff. But he was good to me. He'd take me around in his car and help me pick up cans. He said I was the only person that he could trust. His dad beat him. Bet you didn't know that. Used to put cigarettes out on Tommy's arms; said it would make him tough. Wasn't even his real dad. His mom treated him like shit." Tears welled up in Chuck's eyes. "Nobody cared. Nobody. The teachers, they called him worthless and said he wouldn't amount to much. The kids called him a retard 'cause he had trouble learning." Chuck took a few dollars from his pocket and gave it to Larry. "I'm paying for your lunch today, cuzz. The rest of you assholes can go to hell."

"Yeah, Chucky," Bobby said, "we'll tell Tommy you said hello when we get there."

Chuck yelled, "You chicken-shit mother-fucker!" He leapt at Bobby, putting him in a choke—hold. Larry sprang up and grabbed Chuck's hands and pried them loose from Bobby's neck, then forced him outside.

Bobby was bent over in his chair struggling for air.

Sill heard the commotion and ran from the kitchen. She saw Bobby choking and went over to help. "You okay, Bobby?" She asked.

Bobby struggled for a breath, shook his head 'yes' and held up a finger as if to say 'just give me a moment.'

Sill held his shoulder with one hand and rubbed his back with the other. "Relax, Bobby, it'll come back." She assured. "Betsy, go get me a glass of water," she ordered.

"Looks like Larry's walking Chucky to the trailer," Duck said, now standing and looking out the window. "Grump, this would have never happened if you . . ."

"It's not Grump's fault," Paul interrupted. "Bobby was being nice to Chucky for once and Chucky snapped."

"Paul, Bobby is never nice to Chucky," Duck said, walking towards Paul. "He should have kept his mouth shut, just like you should do."

"Listen old man," Paul said, standing up, "if it's been a while since you've had your ass kicked maybe you're due."

"Fellas!" Sill yelled. "Settle down. Duck go back to your seat."

Duck pointed at Paul and exclaimed, "If you'd spend as much time running your business as you spend in here, you wouldn't have to file bankruptcy!" Duck's chin was quivering, and was within reaching distance of Paul.

Paul gritted his teeth and pulled his fist back while simultaneously grabbing the front of Duck's shirt. Sill rushed to put her arm between them, "Knock it off," she cried.

Larry re-entered the diner and saw what was happening. "What's going on here?" He quickly took Sill by the arm and pulled her away, then grabbed Paul. "Paul. Paul. You don't want to do this buddy. You know you'll hurt him bad. It's not worth the trouble. You have enough as it is."

Paul's breathing increased. He looked at Larry, gritted his teeth and grunted loudly, and at the same time let go of Duck with a small shove. Duck caught himself on the table where Bobby was now breathing fine and had lit a cigarette.

"Duck," Bobby said, "you mess with the bull you'll get the horns."

Duck straightened his shirt and returned to his seat.

"You okay Duck?" Ed asked.

Duck shook his head and took a drink of coffee.

Paul slammed the front door as he left. He backed his tow truck out onto Route 268 and punched the accelerator, leaving smoke billowing in the air and black marks beside the ones Tommy had made a few days earlier.

"I think you all need more fiber in your diets," Grump said, chuckling.

Larry returned to his table. Bobby was rubbing his neck, "That little bastard cousin of yours has a hell of a grip."

"It runs in the family," Larry said.

"Don't worry, Big Larr, I won't be starting trouble with you."

"You know you shouldn't have said that to him. That was uncalled for."

Bobby shook his head in agreement, took out another cigarette and lit it on the dying one in his hand.

Sill took a fresh pot of coffee and distributed refills. As she refilled Duck's, she lowered her eyebrows and gave him a scolding look. She whispered, "How did you know he filed bankruptcy, eh?"

Duck lowered his head and mumbled, "I looked in the garbage, like Jill did."

Sill held out her empty hand.

Duck gave her an inquisitive look.

"The key," she said.

Duck's eyes grew bigger, like a kid who just had his best toy taken away, about to cry.

"The key, Duck. You'll have to earn it back."

He slowly took a key ring from his pocket and removed the Rose Bud key and put it in Sill's hand.

She closed her hand around it and walked away to finish the refills.

"Well," said Ray, wanting to raise everyone's spirits, "did I ever tell all you fine people the story about my mother's great, great uncle going into business with John Wilkes Booth?"

"Who's that?" Betsy asked.

"They guy who killed George Washington," Grump said with a chuckle.

"Oh," Betsy said. "Did you guys know George Washington slept a night on one of the islands in Parker?"

"Yes." Jim said.

"Oh," Betsy said.

"Anyway," Ray interrupted, "my mother's great, great uncle was LeRoy Montgomery Majors. He was a businessman from Cleveland. Uh, that's in Ohio, Betsy."

"I know," Betsy replied.

"Just wanted to make sure," Ray said, and was now standing as he had done several times like he was lecturing a class. "Well, anyway, LeRoy sold one of his businesses and was looking for an investment. This was about the time of the oil boom up in Venango County. One evening he went to the theatre in Cleveland, as was the custom of the wealthy at that time. And there was a young actor there by the name of John Wilkes Booth, who captured the attention of LeRoy. Having a position of influence with the owner of the theatre, LeRoy was able to get backstage after the play to meet Mr. Booth. Following a lengthy conversation LeRoy learned that Mr. Booth was looking to make investments with his new found fame and fortune. To make a long story short . . ."

"Thank God," Grump said.

Ray lowered his eyebrows towards Grump and continued. "LeRoy and one of his business partners took Mr. Booth to Venango County to investigate possible land purchases for drilling oil wells. This was 1863, just two years before the infamous assassination. In any event, they formed what was called the Dramatic Oil Company and purchased three and a half acres of land from the Fuller Farm near Franklin."

"Benjamin Franklin?" Betsy asked.

"Uh, no, my dear, Franklin, Pennsylvania."

"Oh."

"Uh, anyway," Ray continued, "the investment paid nice dividends to the three gentlemen, and was churning along nicely until Mr. Booth committed his crime. LeRoy and his friend were investigated because of their affiliation with the murderer. LeRoy swore he knew nothing about it. But in these parts back then, as beloved as Abraham Lincoln was, the mere affiliation with Booth was cause for banishment. LeRoy never returned to Venango County and sold the business, which later, in 1913 I believe, was one of the original nineteen oil companies brought together by Charles Pape of Chicago to form the Quaker State Oil Company." Ray finished with a smile, "and there you have it," and sat down.

"Well, I'll be . . ." Grump said. "Finally, something interesting spewed from your yapper, Ray."

"I'll take that as a compliment, Grump." Ray replied.

"Holy shit, Ray, you could have been an heir to the Quaker State fortune. Sum-bitch." Bobby added.

"Well, Bobby, I never count chickens I've never owned."

June 9, Wednesday—Dizzy

8:10 AM

Betsy came in early to help Sill pick up the slack for what Duck normally did.

"Why did you take Duck's key, Sill?" Betsy asked.

"It's a long story, Betsy. I really don't want to talk about it."

"Oh," Betsy said. "What's next?"

"Make a pot of decaf for Duck and take the garbage out from last night."

The whole gang was there except for Paul and Chuck.

"Anybody know where I can find a tail light cover for a '64 Ford Falcon?" Jim asked.

"Did you call Paul?" Bobby asked.

"Yeah," Jim replied, "But there was no answer last night."

"How about Hovis in Emlenton?" Grump added.

"They don't have one," Jim answered.

"I think Hobaugh in Karns City might have one. I saw them towing in a Falcon yesterday afternoon when I was taking mom to the doctor in Butler. I don't know what year it was though." Ed said.

"Thanks Ed," Jim said.

"Funny about Paul. He's probably still pissed off at Duck." Bobby said and took a drag on his cigarette. "Betsy, more coffee, babe!"

Betsy walked over to Bobby. Her shirt revealed a stout cleavage and was cut just short enough to expose the bottom edge of her belly button. Her jeans were tight and hugged a firm carriage. She bent over to refill Bobby's coffee. His eyes were firmly planted on the droop in her shirt. He took a deep breath of her perfume. "Sweetheart," he whispered, "If you weren't jail bait I'd show you the sleeper cab in my truck."

Betsy giggled, "Bobby, Bobby, Bobby. You dirty old man."

"I'm not old, sweetheart." He said, "These guys are old," pointing to the room.

Betsy made her rounds with the coffee, flirted, and returned to the kitchen.

"That'll get you into trouble, you know." Larry said quietly to Bobby.

"Yeah, I know. But just one time. Just one time. Man. Wow." Bobby said. He took a drag and blew the smoke to the ceiling, then flicked his ash into the ashtray. He bent toward Larry and whispered, "Wow."

"Boy she's a good looker," Grump said.

"You wouldn't know what to do with that," Duck said.

"Yeah," Bobby said, "Grump, you'd blow a nut and pass out before the first kiss."

"You guys are sick." Jill said on her way to the bathroom.

"You ain't so bad yourself, Jilly Pilly." Bobby said.

Jill gave him the bird.

"Okay!" Bobby said. "You name the place and time and I'll be there."

"Only in your dreams, buddy." Jill said.

"Hey Ed," Duck asked, "what does the Bible say about temptation?"

"It says that God will provide a way out." Ed responded.

"He didn't provide a way out for King David," Jim said.

"I didn't know you knew so much about the Bible," Ed said.

"You never asked," Jim replied.

"David and Bath-something," Duck said.

"Bathsheba," Grump said.

"Grump," Ed said, "I'm surprised you know so much about the Bible."

"I'm a fan of history. It's a good history book." Grump said.

"Actually," Ray said, "there is some archeological evidence that proves the existence of many places and characters in the Bible. Grump is right; it is history. So, if we are going to accept that the Bible to historically true, we therefore have to say that it is spiritually true also. The tumbled walls of Jericho were found just as the Bible says they were. That's not happenstance or coincidence, Grump."

Grump took a sip of coffee to wash down the toast with smooth peanut butter. "Ok, but there's no historical evidence of Jesus."

"He was real, Grump." Ed said.

"Prove it," Grump replied.

"Uh, actually, gentlemen," Ray said, "the Roman historian Publius Cornelius Tacitus and the Jewish historian Josephus both wrote of Jesus."

"Did you say Pubic?" Bobby asked Ray, chuckling.

Betsy heard it and laughed out loud. Bobby winked at her.

"See Grump, there's your historical evidence," Ed said.

"Yes," Ray said, "They both write that there was a leader named Jesus, he was executed, and the movement he started survived his death."

"I have a movement about to start," Bobby said on his way to the bathroom. Jill was coming out as he entered, "Hey darling, everything come out okay?"

"You're ignorant," Jill replied, slapping him on the shoulder.

Grump scratched his chin, "That's not evidence. Those guys were probably converted Christians."

"Well, actually, Grump," Ray said, "Tacitus detested Christians and Jews; and Josephus was Jewish and there's no evidence that he ever converted to Christianity."

"There you have it, Grump. Jesus was real, and still is." Ed replied.

"Well, actually, Ed," Ray continued, "There's no evidence that Jesus was God except if you believe what the Bible says."

Ed looked at Ray, "You said earlier that if we accept that the Bible is historically true, then it is spiritually true also."

"I did?" Ray said, rubbing his forehead.

"Yes, you did." Ed replied.

"You okay Ray?" Duck asked.

"I'm a little dizzy." Ray replied.

"Catch him!" Duck yelled.

Ray's eyes rolled back and he was falling from his chair. Grump reached over and grabbed his shoulder but was unable to stop him. Larry, who had turned his chair around to hear Ray's lecture, sprung all four hundred pounds towards Ray and caught him before he hit the floor. "Sill, call and ambulance," Larry yelled.

"Oh my God," Jill said. She ran to get a cold rag to put on Ray's forehead.

"Give me your hat, Jim." Larry said. He put the hat between Ray's head and the hard floor.

"The Rose Bud. Up on the hill." Sill said into the phone. "Hold on . . . ," she put the phone down and walked into the dining area. "Is Ray conscious?"

"No." Larry said.

Sill ran back to the phone. "No, he's not. Okay. Okay. I hear the sirens now. I'm going out to help. Bye."

Ray opened his eyes. Jill was rubbing his forehead with the cold rag. "Hey, Jilly Pilly," he said softly. He looked at Larry, "Did you slug me?" he asked, evoking mild laughter from everyone.

The ambulance crew arrived and swept Ray to the hospital. They put an oxygen mask on his face, lifted him onto a rolling gurney and loaded him into the ambulance.

"I'll walk over and drive his wife to the hospital," Larry said.

June 10, Thursday—Caffeine and Racism (Two things we could all do without.)

8:00 A.M.

The whole crew was there except for Paul and Chuck.

"Anybody hear from Ray?" Duck asked.

"I called his house last night and talked to him," Larry said.

"What's the deal?" Grump asked.

"Caffeine," Larry said.

"Caffeine?" Grump asked.

"Yeah, the doctors said he had too much caffeine and it restricted the blood vessels in his head so much that it caused a lack of oxygen to the brain."

"He only drank two cups," Duck said.

"Well, according to his wife, he gets up at 4:00 AM every morning and drinks four or five cups before he comes over here."

"Holy crap," Duck said. "I'll have to make sure we serve him decaf from now on."

The front door opened and Ray walked in, "Howdy fellas! Did you miss me?"

"Hey Ray," they all said in unison.

"Speak of the devil and he shall arise," said Bobby.

"Caffeine, huh?" said Duck.

"Yep," said Ray. "Where's the coffee?" He said, snickering.

"Sit down, Ray, I'll get you some decaf," Duck said.

Ray started into a lecture before he sat down. "You know gentlemen, caffeine is a funny chemical. It has a half-life of six hours in the body. That means if you drink one cup of coffee now, only half of it will be out of your system in six hours. I was drinking so much of it, it was never able to leave my body totally."

"Just glad to see you're okay, Ray," Larry said.

"Oh, and thanks Larry for bringing the Mrs. to the hospital yesterday. I really appreciate that. Oh, and Jilly, thanks for taking care of me with that cold rag. It felt so good I didn't want you to stop."

"No problem, Ray bird," as she patted him on the back.

"Well," said Ray, "now that you've got me back, what do you want to talk about?"

"You got any good jokes?" Bobby asked.

"Well, let's see . . . here's one . . . a ham sandwich walked into the bar and asked for a beer. To which the bartender replied, 'Sorry, we don't serve food here.'"

"Hey, that's not bad." Duck said. "Hey, here's one . . . somebody ask me if I'm Elvis Presley."

"What?" Jim said.

"Ask me if I'm Elvis Presley," Duck replied.

"Ok," Jim said, "I'll bite. Are you Elvis Presley?"

Duck snickered, "No."

Ray busted out laughing, but nobody else did. "That's a good one, Duck. Did you make that up?"

"Some kid down at Whyte's told it to me. I thought it was a good one too."

"It's the stupidest damn joke I've ever heard," Bobby said.

"Okay then, Mr. Entertainer, you tell one." Duck said, looking at Bobby.

"How many niggers does it take to tar a road?" Bobby said.

Silence. Ray shook his head in disapproval.

"Three—if you spread them thin." Bobby yelled, laughing.

Grump managed a chuckle.

"My best friend in Seminary was black." Ed said.

"Well," Bobby declared, "if you want to socialize with them porch monkeys, you go right ahead. Can't understand a goddamn word they say on the CB anyway."

"Bobby," Ray said softly, "I taught many fine, intelligent African Americans. You must have had a bad experience at some point and now you don't like any of them."

"Yeah," Bobby interrupted, "I had plenty of bad experiences with them. Them sum-bitches band together like sheep. Just last year I had two of them try to rob me blind at a truck stop in West Virginia."

Grump chuckled. "You should have seen them in the war. They had their own division. Couldn't trust any of them."

"Grump," Duck said, "what's the name of that fellow you buy your tomato starts from in Butler?"

"Why?"

"Well, isn't he a black man?"

"Yeah, Jesus Christ, but he's different."

"How is he different?" Ray asked.

"He's just different." Grump replied.

"So," said Ray, "do you trust him?"

"Just shut up and eat your damn breakfast." Grump said.

"We're all made in the image of God." Ed added.

"God ain't black," Grump said.

"God doesn't know color, Grump," Ed replied, "He just looks at the heart."

"I ain't going to sit here with no damn coon sympathizers." Bobby declared.

"And I ain't going to sit here with a racist." Duck replied.

"Bobby," Ray said, "My daughter married a black man and you know what? I don't even see his color anymore. He's just my son-in-law."

"Yeah," Bobby said, "I heard stories about that. Said he's got a dick bigger than a telephone pole and lips wider than the Allegheny. I bet your daughter enjoys that."

Larry looked at Bobby, "Now that's totally uncalled for. You need to apologize to Ray."

"Screw you, ya big baboon. I ain't apologizing to nobody." Bobby said.

Ray got up and walked into the kitchen.

Larry leaned over and whispered to Bobby, "Listen, you hurt that old man. You need to leave because the more you act like a dickhead the angrier I get. And you don't want me to get angry, fella."

Bobby blew a puff of smoke in Larry's face and extinguished his cigarette. He threw ten dollars on the table, "That's for mine and Ray's breakfast. Tell the old man I'm sorry," and walked out.

Larry went into the kitchen to see how Ray was doing. "Where's Ray," he asked Sill.

She pointed back to her office. Ray was sitting there with his head in one hand and squeezing his knee with the other. Larry knocked lightly on the wall, "Hey Ray, how ya doin'?"

He looked up at Larry with sad eyes. "Why do people have to hate?" He asked. "Life is too short to hate. When you compare the amount of time we are on this earth to the age of the universe, we practically don't exist. There's no time for hate, Larry."

Larry leaned against the doorway. "I agree, Ray. When my wife left, I hated her until I could learn to let her go. In the end, I wanted her to be happy, even if it was with another man. In a perverted sort of way, I guess, that's how I showed my love for her, by letting her go."

"That's beautiful, Larry," Ray said.

"Listen Ray, Bobby just left. You are welcome to come back out and join us. Nobody is going to talk about this anymore."

"Thanks Larry, but that's okay. I think I'm just gonna go home for now. I'll slip out the back. Here's a few dollars for my breakfast. Give it to Sill for me, would you?"

"Bobby already paid for your breakfast."

Ray's eyes grew bigger, "Well, that's a start."

"Yeah," Larry said, "that's his way of apologizing to you."

"I'll be okay tomorrow, Larry. I learned a long time ago not to hold grudges."

"No grudges. No caffeine. Got it." Larry said with a smile.

Ray smiled back, "You're one of the good ones, Larry. Salt of the earth."

Larry smiled and threw Ray a quick salute.

June 14th, Monday—Trouble, Oh Deer and Split Pea Soup

Chuck walked in and sat at his booth.

"What's up Chuck?" Bobby asked.

Chuck grunted.

"Vomit. Get it? Upchuck." Bobby laughed.

"Leave him alone. He had a rough time of it lately." Larry said.

"I've had lots of rough times." Bobby replied, "One night I had five hundred miles to go to get home and I stopped and picked up a hitch hiker. Turns out he had a gun and held me at gunpoint and told me to drive to Detroit. The bastard said he wanted me to take him through the tunnel under the Detroit River into Windsor, Canada. From there he said he'd let me go. I told the crazy bastard I couldn't go through that tunnel without a permit.

"I had to drive from Charlotte, North Carolina to Detroit. When we stopped to take a leak or get fuel he'd tell me that if I tried anything he'd kill me. So I didn't try any funny stuff. Long story short, we got to the entrance of the tunnel and they asked me for my permit to pass through.

"When I told them I didn't have one they looked at me like I was crazy. Traffic was backing up behind me and there was little room to turn around. I figured the time was now or never to escape. In one quick motion I turn off the truck, took the keys, opened the door and jumped out.

"The officers pounced on me and held me down. I told them that I was kidnapped and the guy in the truck had a gun. They still handcuffed me and sat me against their little guard building.

"They drew their guns and told the bastard to get out of the truck. He just sat there. Then I heard them say 'put the gun down.' Then I saw him get out holding the gun to his head. He said he's going through that tunnel or he'd kill himself. And he started to walk into the tunnel with guards following him with their guns drawn.

"I don't know what ever happened to that bastard. The last thing I saw was him walking into the tunnel with the gun pointed to his head. I hope he pulled the damn trigger."

"That's quite a story," Ed said. "When I was a kid my parents planted acres and acres of strawberry plants. I'd have to spread the straw on the rows of plants and every night after school we'd have to carry buckets of water from the house to the fields, about a 100 yard walk.

"When the strawberries were ready to be picked my father would wake us up at 4:00 AM before school and out we'd go to the field. It was wet and chilly. We'd take buckets and stagger them down the rows and fill them up. I remember my lower back getting really sore. It would hurt so much I'd get down on my knees in the mud, even though I knew my father would give me a whipping for getting my school clothes dirty. I had two pairs of pants—one for church and one for school. If I got them dirty doing chores or playing outside, I'd get a whipping.

"My father used to put me on the horse to plow the field. It was hot and I'd ask for a drink. He said I wasn't working hard enough to deserve a drink. I'd ride that horse for four hours without shade or water. I laid down once over it's neck and grab the mane so I wouldn't fall off. My father took his belt off and beat it across my back and told me to sit up. At lunch time I'd get a sandwich and one glass of water. The horse got oats and water. I felt sorry for that old fellow. It's like we both got through the punishment together. We were buddies. And, of course, my pants got soaked from the horse sweating, and father would refuse to let mother wash them. I'd have to go to school smelling like a horse. It's like my father took pride in making me suffer. Why wouldn't he let mother wash my pants more than once a week? I never understood that."

"I understand it," Grump said. "It's because he came through the depression and it messed people up in the head. My uncle was the same way. My dad died when I was twelve, and my mom didn't want me anymore, so my uncle took me in. Not out of love, mind you. He worked me to the bone. I had to wash dishes, sweep the floors, mow the yard with a rotary manual mower—he couldn't afford a gas-powered mower, back then they were a luxury. I had to feed the dog and make sure he got a bath once a week. He was an outside dog, so he stunk to high heaven. I grew to hate that thing, and I hated my uncle.

"I had to work in the garden pulling weeds. Sometimes I wouldn't mind it because I'd find Indian arrowheads. I started a collection. I had over a hundred. He took it and traded for a gas-powered mower. He said it was to make my life a little easier. But the son-of-a-bitch made me walk five miles to get gas for it. I'd rather have kept the arrowhead collection."

"Damn, that sucks you guys," Chuck said. "I thought I had it rough. I have to scavenge for cans and glass. Last night mom got sick and I had to take care of her."

"Sorry to hear that," Ed said.

"That's okay, Ed. She's better. I didn't get much sleep though. I came over here to get a break."

Split Pea Soup

"After I lost my wife," Duck said, "it was tough going for awhile. She did all the cooking, cleaning and grocery shopping. I didn't know how to do those things, but I soon learned.

"She made split pea soup like nobody's business. She'd take a ham hock and simmer it in water for a couple hours, then she'd put the split peas in and in a few more hours she'd have the best split pea soup this side of the Mississippi.

"I decided that I'd try to make split pea soup like she did. I went to the store and bought a ham hock and some split peas. I took it home and put the water on to simmer in a big pot. I got the water boiling and put in the ham hock, then turned the heat down to simmer. I let it go for an hour and tasted it. It was too weak. I put too much water in. So I threw in some salt and beef bullion cubes because that's all I had and I don't think they make ham bullion. I'll have to ask Sill. Anywho, I let it simmer for another hour. It tasted a little strong so I poured out some of the water and replaced it with fresh water. It simmered again and finally I got it to taste okay.

"I poured in three bags of split peas. It sure doesn't look like much when it's in the bag. I put the lid on and turned the heat way down and went in the room.

"I watched TV for a while, read the paper and fell asleep. I was dreaming about Niagara Falls. It was a beautiful sight. The spray coming up out of the pit sure made a sound like water boiling over a pot and hitting the burner.

"I woke up and still heard that sound. Damn! The soup! I ran out to the kitchen and what a mess! The peas had swollen and filled the pot. The lid popped up and the peas oozed over the top and down onto the stove. It must have been doing this for a while because the peas filled up the pit underneath the burner and then oozed down onto the floor. They soaked up enough water in the pot to cause them to burn on the bottom about an inch thick."

Small laughter rang around the room and settled.

Oh Deer!

"You going hunting this year Jim?" Larry asked.

"Probably so," Jim said, "It depends on how much work I have. Business is usually slower in the winter."

"You won the buck pool last year, didn't you?" Larry asked.

"Yeah. I got lucky. I was down in Barger Hollow in my tree stand and he was following two doe. When he got underneath me I whistled and he stopped and I plugged him through the front shoulders. That was the nicest deer I ever shot. Don't think I'll ever top that one."

"I hit a big buck with my truck last year. Sum-bitch smashed my grill." Bobby added.

"I missed one last year back on the Kaufman farm and Grump wanted to cut my shirt tail off." Duck said.

Grump laughed. "You couldn't hit the broad side of a barn if you were standing inside it."

"I took my grandson hunting last year. That's the last time I'll ever do that." Ed said. "He couldn't sit still and he complained constantly—'I'm cold, I'm hungry, I have to go to the bathroom.'"

"I took my grandson hunting last year too." Grump said. "He was the same way. He wanted to go back to the house at ten o'clock. We were sitting on an old log, back to back. I told him to switch places with me, hoping the new scenery would keep him occupied for a while. Lo and behold, he yelled 'here they come Grandpa' and the next thing I heard was his gun roaring. I stood up and looked down the hill. All I saw was two doe running away, white tails flickering. The first thing I thought was, *the little bastard shot a doe.* I asked him if he's sure he got a buck. 'Sure Grandpa. I think,' he said. We ran down the hill and there it was, a nice six point, but it was still alive and trying to get up. I reached down and unfastened my knife to slit its throat. Then I heard his gun roar again. The little sum-bitch walked over and shot it in the head and cracked one of the horns at the base. 'Can't mount it now,' I told him. I handed him the knife and told him to gut it out. 'I don't know how,' he said. I had to gut that thing. It was his first deer so I showed him how to do it. I cut the stink bags off its legs and started up the belly. He watched me cut its nuts and peter off and I held them up to him. He just said 'yuck.' I told him they were good eating," Grumped laughed. "He wouldn't reach in and pull the guts out or even the heart. I did it all. I told him I ain't dragging the son-of-a-bitch out of the woods. It took him an hour to go one hundred feet, but he got it out of there."

"That reminds me of a story about my nephew," Jim said. "We took the kids and my nephew Wesley out to Akron, Ohio to see their great uncle, and he decided it would be a nice idea to take the kids to a petting zoo. We got some pellets and went in with the deer. I gave some to Wesley and I turned around to feed a big buck. The next thing I know I hear Wesley screaming. He went over by himself to feed a fawn. I guess the mother didn't like it so much so she came over and attacked him. When I looked over, she was on top of him clubbing his chest with her front hooves. Poor kid. I think he's hated deer ever since. He wasn't hurt bad. A few bruises and scratches."

"Oh deer!" Duck said with a chuckle.

June 15th, Tuesday— Another Joke Day

8:15 A.M.

"Anybody got any jokes?" Bobby asked.

"It's too damn early for jokes," Paul muttered.

"Yeah, I got one," Grump said, "what does a walrus and Tupperware have in common?"

No answer.

"They both like a tight seal." Grump said, chuckling.

"Oh, I got one." Duck said. "This ham sandwich walked into a bar and ordered a beer. The bartender said 'sorry, we don't serve food here.'"

Nobody laughed.

"You told that one ten times before, Duck. It's getting old," Bobby said. "Here's one I heard on the road the other day."

"Keep it nice," Larry interrupted.

Bobby looked at Larry and took a drag on his cigarette and blew it to the ceiling, "Did you hear about the confused bank robber?" He started to laugh and could barely finish the joke, "He . . . he . . . he tied up the safe and . . . and . . . blew the guard."

Betsy busted out laughing, nearly spilling a tray of food. Grump nearly choked on his coffee. And even Ed chuckled.

"I got one," Jim said. "Why was six afraid of seven?"

In unison, they all answered, "Because seven ate nine."

"Jim, do you know another joke to tell. That one is older than Moses," Ray said.

"Hey," Grump said, "how many Pollocks does it take to screw in a light bulb? Three . . . one to hold the light bulb and two to turn the ladder."

70

A few chuckles resulted.

"That's an old one," Larry said.

"I got another one," Bobby said. "Why do blacks hate whites?"

Everyone froze, afraid of the answer. Nobody wanted to prompt Bobby for the punch line. Nobody wanted a repeat of last Thursday's debacle.

"Because they're white and they work," Bobby continued.

Grump was the only one that chuckled.

"I have a joke," Ray said, "wanting to move quickly beyond what he had just heard. "Two hydrogen molecules are walking along a street. The first one says, 'Hey! I think I lost an electron!' To which the second one replies, 'Are you sure?' The first one then says, 'Yeah, I'm POSITIVE!'"

Nobody got it but Ray, who could barely contain his laughter.

June 16th, Wednesday—Grump's Speech, Duck's Story, Douche Gel and Bucky Jones

Grump arrived late to the Rose Bud.

"Where you been?" Bobby asked.

Grump didn't answer. He walked to his table where Jim, Ed and Ray were already seated. He motioned to Jill for a cup of coffee.

Duck saw Grump like this before and recognized the situation. There was a bad thunderstorm the night before and sometimes the thunder was so loud it took Grump back to the war. It took him at least a day to get over it. Meantime, he retreated inside himself until it all passed.

"You guys need to leave Grump alone today. He doesn't feel good." Duck said.

"Grump, if you're sick, go home. We don't want it. And I can't afford to miss a day of work," Bobby said.

Duck quickly responded, "Bobby, if you're here every day, when the hell do you work?"

"I'm a short-haul driver now, asshole. I start at 2:00 PM and get home at midnight."

"Oh," Duck said. "Anyway, Grump's not sick-sick, it's just that the thunderstorm last night shook him up a little."

"You got shell shock Grump?" Bobby asked.

Grump looked at Bobby, as if to stare right through him.

"Sorry, Grump," Bobby said, and then lit a cigarette.

There was a respectful calm for a few minutes.

"Fellas," Grump said, breaking the silence, "I'm going to tell you this story once and only once. I don't know why I'm telling you this. I guess because it's time to tell it."

"You don't have to talk about it, Grump," Larry offered.

"I don't know why, but I feel like I have to get this off my chest," Grump explained.

Grump described the day he hit Omaha Beach at Normandy.

"Every June I take myself through the events of that day. It was June 6th, 1944. We left the ship in the LCVP landing craft. It was the beginning of Operation Overlord. You guys know it as D-Day. I was one of the oldest ones on board—thirty-five. I begged them to take me in 1941 when I went to the enlistment office. They turned me away for having flat feet, but I kept going back. I think they got tired of seeing me, so they signed me up. I wanted to serve my country, even if it meant leaving my wife and children.

"They shipped me to England to prepare for the invasion, but at the time they didn't tell us what we were there for. It was 5:30 AM and the fog was thick and the coast of England faded behind us. We felt like we were alone. The Sergeant told us to make peace with God because many of us could be meeting him soon.

"After what seemed like an eternity, it was time. The diesel engine from the landing craft drowned out most of the mortar fire on shore, but the closer we got the louder it became. My breathing grew heavy and I was scared shitless. I was one of the lucky ones that was loaded into the craft first, which meant I was in the back, away from the landing gate.

"The fog burnt off by 6:00 A.M. and we were close enough to smell gun powder and smoke coming from the beach. The lid under my right eye started to twitch uncontrollably. The guy next to me was praying and someone else threw up on my boots. Sarge yelled, 'two minutes,' and right then I felt the craft come to a jolting halt. Turns out we lit on a sand bar about a hundred yards offshore. The coxswain tried like hell to get it off. We'd be sitting ducks if he couldn't get it out of there. He yelled at the Sarge to put a few of us over the side to lighten the load. By now we could hear bullets clinking against the sides and I could see dents inside the landing gate from the German fifty calibers.

"I didn't think about it. I threw off my pack and gun and jumped over the side. The water was well over my head so I rolled over and floated on my back. I was a strong swimmer. I used to swim across the Allegheny when I was a kid, then turn around and swim back. About ten of the guys followed me over the side. A few of them forgot to throw off their packs and when they hit the water they sank like rocks. I dove down and saved one of them.

"We got enough men off the LCVP that it was light enough to get off the sand bar. The coxswain reversed the engines and stopped the boat long enough that we could swim over and climb back in. One of the guys took a bullet and fell back into the sea. I wanted to jump in and get him but Sarge said to stay put, he was dead.

"I was wet, cold and scared. And I wanted nothing to do with that beach. All I could think about was a hot bowl of soup and a warm bed. The bullets forced me abruptly back to reality. I forgot to crouch and I heard one zing over my head. If you've ever had a bullet zing over your head when you were out hunting, just multiply that by ten. The Germans were using fifty caliber machine guns on portable turrets.

"The closer we got to the beach the better angle the Germans had from the top of the cliff, about one hundred seventy feet high. They started lobbing artillery shells at us from behind the concrete bunkers. The boat beside us took a direct hit.

"'Thirty seconds, lock and load,' I heard Sarge yell. We all stood up and the coxswain unlatched the landing gate. We jumped out into three feet of red water. Ten of our guys were taken out before they could reach the edge of the sand. I ran about forty feet and dove behind a hedgehog. Those were the things that looked like giant steel jumping jacks stuck in the sand. Bullets were tinking off the hedgehog and some of them were hitting the sand at my feet. Those bastards had every square inch of that beach pre-sighted. No place was safe.

"I figured if I stayed behind that hedgehog, one of those bullets would find me sooner or later. I peaked around the steel and saw a row of barbed wire about thirty yards ahead of me. Just before that was a pit from a mortar shell. Another guy was in it but it looked like there was room for one more. I rolled quickly to my right and ran like a deer, zig zagging, and dove into the pit. I said something to that guy. I rolled him over and his face had been blown off. I took his body and laid it in front of the pit for cover. What I didn't know at the time is that I had just run through a minefield. That's why nobody was following me. I was alone, except for my newfound friend in the pit."

By now, everyone was turned toward Grump, listening to every syllable. He asked for a glass of water. Sill ran into the kitchen for it, wanting him to get back to the story as quickly as possible. Grump took a drink and continued.

"I used my friend as a shield as I took short peaks to see how things were laid out. I could see Sarge to the north of me, screaming at guys to get off the beach and up to the base of the sea wall. They were getting picked off like it was turkey season. Mortal shells were raining onto every position. I could see a pillbox at the top of the cliff with two machine guns ripping up the beach. I took a bead just above the fire coming out of the barrel on the right and put a round into it. It stopped momentarily; then started again. I took aim and fired again. It stopped permanently that time. Then I took a bead on the other gun and fired. It stopped too. This gave Sarge enough time to get bangalures under the rows of barbed wire and split a hole up to the sea wall.

"The machine guns started again. And once again, having the best angle for shooting, I took aim and took them out. One of the Krauts spotted me and trimmed his machine gun in my direction. I ducked behind my friend and I could hear the bullets piercing his body. I curled up in the hole and I was able to get low enough to cut off the angle. This gave the guys enough time to make it up to the sea wall.

"I was trapped. One of the mines was exposed beside my pit. If a bullet was to hit it just right, I'd be a goner. I decided that the only way out was to go back the way I came in, then follow Sarge's path to the sea wall.

"My tracks were hard to follow in the sand, and I couldn't walk them because I was running when I made them, so they were too far apart; and I'd get picked off if I went too slow. But luck that day came in the form of a few mortar shells.

"A Kraut in one of the mortar pits on the edge of the cliff spotted me. He started lobbing mortar shells at me. Luckily the son-of-a-bitch was a bad aim. I jumped from where I was into a fresh hole. By then he had readjusted to the old hole and had to adjust again to the one I was in. He hit about ten yards away, towards Sarge. I thought to myself *'what the hell'* and ran towards Sarge. I jumped over a small mortar hole and kept running. Sarge saw me coming and had a couple guys jump out from the sea wall and lay down covering fire. Another stroke of luck came to me about then.

"One of our war ships was lobbing artillery onto the top of the cliff. One of the shells hit the pillbox that was shooting at me and simultaneously took out the guy that was lobbing mortars at me. The guys in that ship saved my life, and hundreds of others, and I don't even know who they were.

"We reached the sea wall but, believe it or not, the toughest part was still ahead. We had to negotiate the shelf between the sea wall and the cliff. It ran about a hundred yards to the base of the cliff. The Germans laced it with minefields and barbed wire, and trained their machine guns from positions that would create interlocking fire. Beyond that we would have to negotiate the cliff wall; and then we'd have to fight the enemy hand-to-hand."

Grump stopped talking, as if to say 'that's enough for now.' He took a drink of water and took a deep breath.

"You okay, Grump?" Duck asked.

Grump shook his head in affirmation.

"Holy shit, Grump." Bobby said, "what a story. What happened next?"

Grump took another deep breath, "No more today, Bobby. No more today."

Bobby snuffed out his cigarette and lit another.

Duck's Story

Bobby looked out the window and took a drag from his cigarette. "There goes those damn coal trucks," he said, "putting pot holes in the roads, and our tax dollars have to fix them up again."

"You drive truck Bobby," Duck said, "and yours is bigger. You probably do more damage than theirs."

"I drive mostly Interstate 80, Duck. These guys travel all the side roads that aren't built for that kind of weight."

"I thought you were a short-haul driver," Duck added.

"Are you stupid?" Bobby asked. "I short haul to Cleveland every afternoon and back. That's Interstate 80 and some of 90 all the way."

Duck's face turned red and he pointed his finger at Bobby, "Don't call me stupid, young man. I might be old, but I can still kick your ass."

Bobby laughed, "Maybe. But I doubt it."

"Bobby," Larry interjected, wanting peace, "I bet those coal trucks do a lot of damage to our roads. How in the heck do they get away with it?"

Bobby took a drag and blew it to the ceiling, "Well, they bond those roads before the coal is transported. If they don't fix the road the state cashes the bonds and fixes it."

"Bobby, what the hell do you know about the coal industry anyway," Duck asked.

Bobby rolled his eyes.

"Duck retired from the coal mines, Bobby." Larry said.

"What mines did you work in, Duck?" Jim asked.

"Most of the ones around here."

"Did you ever work at the Monterey mines?" Jim continued.

"Yep."

"Did you know my grandpa?"

"Joseph Radaker?" Duck asked.

"Yes." Jim replied.

"Yep."

"Did you know him very well?"

Duck hesitated. "Well, let's just say this. I was with him the day he died."

Jim cocked his head in disbelief, "Really?"

"Yep."

"My mom told me the story of how he died. But I never knew anyone that was with him that day. Tell me what you remember," Jim implored.

"Well, there's really not much to tell you, Jim." Duck said.

"Mom always said there was a guy with him that day but she never knew who it was. Was that you, Duck?"

Duck took a sip of coffee and shook his head in affirmation.

"Wow. I never knew," Jim said. "Can you tell me about what happened?"

"Well, I suppose if you want to hear it," Duck said, "I can tell you. You sure you want everyone else to hear this?"

"I don't mind," Jim said.

"Well," said Duck, "we had just finished our lunch. We took an extra few minutes to rest because for some reason we were both really tired that day. I know why I was tired, actually. I'd been out tipping the bottle the night before. But your grandpa was a devout Christian and he wouldn't do that, so I don't know why he was so tired. I fired up a Cutty Pipe and your pappy laid his head back for a moment and closed his eyes.

"We were both filthy, as you can imagine, and he mentioned that he couldn't wait to get home to take a hot bath and eat your grandma's cooking. I agreed, although my wife wasn't the cook that your grandma was. We both needed a vacation, but that was unheard of back then. We worked six days a week. I sometimes worked seven, but not your pappy. He'd always take Sundays off to go to church and rest.

"I finished my cigarette and he jumped up and said 'Let's go Elmer, we're burning daylight.' As we walked down to the mine entrance he was telling me the story of his new grandson, Jimmy. Said he was a good looker, like him, and he laughed."

Duck looked at Jim and chuckled, "He was talking about you, Jim."

Jim smiled. Ed patted him on the back.

Duck continued. "The last thing he did before going into that mine was stop, look up at the sky and say 'It sure is a beautiful day to be alive.' I agreed and we walked into the mine together and got into a coal car, lit our headlamps, and off we went.

"We got off about a half mile in and walked back to the side shaft where we'd been drilling for the past week. You see, the way you mined back then was, you'd have to leave what you took so the mine wouldn't cave in. If you took a twenty-foot section of coal, you'd leave twenty feet beside it for support.

"Jim, your pappy was the best driller in the business. He knew where to drill and where not to drill. For some reason, he got it wrong that day. I'm thinking because he was just so tired, because he never made a drilling mistake for as long as I knew him. It's like he could feel the coal vein and know its weak and strong points.

"He started into a new vein with the drill. Now this was no drill like you have hanging in your garage. This was a hundred-pound manual auger. He was a strong son of a gun, and he'd push that baby through the coal like it was butter. He'd drill the hole, then the blasters would come in and set the charges and blow out a section of coal. I'd come along with my crew and haul out the pieces; then your pappy would go about his drilling again.

"Sometimes he'd have to crawl back into a narrow shaft, lay on his back and drill into the short ceiling. On that day this is what he was doing. I had a bad feeling about it, but I'd had those before and nothing bad happened. I saw him crawl back in and he got stuck once. I told him to let one of my smaller guys crawl in there and do it. He would have none of it. It was his job to drill and that's what he was going to do.

"He made it back and got the drill in a press position and started into the ceiling. I heard a crack and the drill ground to a stop. I yelled to see if he was okay. He said he was fine. The drill just got stuck and he thought the bit was broken. He struggled to dislodge the drill from the hole, and that's when it happened.

"A large section of rock let loose and came down on him. When they found him the drill had somehow dislodged, spun around and what was left of the bit was driven through his chest. He died instantly, they said."

Jim was staring down at his coffee cup, rubbing the handle with his thumb.

"He was a good man, Jim," Ed assured. "A good man. And a Christian. He's with the Lord now."

"Thank God," said Jim. "Thank God."

Douche Gel

Ray felt an obligation to lighten up the mood. "Did I tell you guys about the time I went to Germany to visit friends and showered with douche gel?" Ray asked.

"What?" Jill asked. "Ray!"

"Just wait, Jilly Pilly, listen to the story. Well, I had a student from Germany in my class. She was so smart and her parents sent her over here to study because they thought American universities had better methods of teaching since they both were educated here and understood our system. Anyway, I met her parents when they came to visit. At graduation they told me to come over sometime to visit and I could stay at their house. Of course I said I would, but never imagined I'd have the time.

"My wonderful wife convinced me one summer to go over, so I made plans and did just that. I flew into Munich and they picked me up there. It was a wonderful time. We went to Neuschwanstein castle, the one that mad King Ludwig of Bavaria built. Then we went to Linderhof castle, Ludwig's playhouse where he had a big smoking room, about as big as this dining room. No Cutty Pipe though, Duck.

Duck chuckled and Ray continued.

"Then they took me to a monastery where I sampled vintage beer. Those monks sure knew how to brew it. They had over a thousand years of practice.

"Anyway, it was my first night in Germany and I was getting ready for bed. I jumped into the shower and couldn't find the soap. I looked around but the only thing I could find was Douche Gel. You can imagine what I was thinking. I took the cap off of it and sniffed. It smelled like perfume. I put some on my finger and rubbed it. It lathered. So I shrugged my shoulders and said 'why not' and put a glob in my palm. I put it on me and lathered up. Not bad for douche gel—must make the ladies of the house smell really good.

"As I described this to the father of the house, he started to laugh—profusely I might add. When he recovered, he said that that was not douche gel. You see, the word 'douche' in German means 'shower.' I was using shower gel, not douche gel."

Jill broke out into uncontrollable laughter and went back to the kitchen to tell Betsy and Sill. A few minutes later there was loud cackle echoing from the kitchen.

Bucky Jones

Larry took a drink of coffee to wash down the remains of a bite of toast and egg. He let out a satisfying "ahhh" and set the cup down. "Any more good stories today? Preferably something positive and reassuring."

"Oh, yes, positive," Ray said, "We haven't had 'positive' around here in a while. Except for my joke, of course." He laughed. Nobody else did.

"What about you, Larry?" Duck asked. "It's been a while since you've told a story. What about the time you were in Korea and saved your buddy's life?"

"He said 'positive,'" Grump added. "And besides, Larry was in Vietnam, not Korea."

"Oh," Duck replied.

"It's okay, Grump. I've got one," Larry said. "It's a little tale about Bucky Jones."

"Who's Bucky Jones?" Duck asked.

"It was a long time ago. We were seniors in high school. Bucky's dad owned Big Buck Tavern in Emlenton. Bucky was next to the youngest of five kids, four boys and a girl. Funny thing about Bucky Jones Sr., he wasn't in favor of naming any of his boys after him, until Bucky came along of course. The story is that when Bucky Jr. was born, Sr. told his wife that this might be the last chance he had to name a Jr. So that's what he did, and the result was Bucky Jones Jr.

"He was pretty stout, like me. Not many kids would mess with us because of our sizes. Believe it or not, there's a little muscle under this four hundred pounds of blubber. Anyway, one day I was visiting Bucky and he told me to follow him upstairs. He took me up to his parents' bedroom and opened the closet door. He pulled back the clothes and there it was—a big, shiny black safe with a big silver dial on it. He said 'watch this,' and began to open it.

"I was getting really nervous because I was afraid of Bucky Sr. I saw him tear into one of Bucky's older brothers one time and he put a hurting on him, and he was the biggest of the bunch, even bigger than the old man. Bucky told me not to worry, that his dad was at the tavern and wouldn't be home for a long time. His mom was at church.

"Bucky opened the safe door and he let me look inside. There was more money in that safe than I'd ever seen. Even now I've never seen so much in one place at the same time. He took out a small bundle and closed the door and spun the dial.

"I asked him what he was doing. He just looked at me and said that we were going to have a good time. We walked down to a restaurant in town and we ate like kings. He also bought me clothes and shoes and then we drove and picked up a couple girls and took them to the movies and had dinner, and we didn't even put a dent in that bundle of cash.

"All was well and good, and then I had a terrible thought come over me. How was I supposed to explain the new clothes and shoes to my parents? I didn't want to lie about it. I told Bucky he put me in a bad position. Now I had to lie to my parents. He told me just to tell them that my parents took us out and treated us to all this stuff. I was worried that my mom would call his mom and we'd be found out. Bucky had an answer for everything. He assured me that his mom was never home, always doing something for the church or playing cards or helping cook at the tavern, so there's no way she'd be home if my mom ever called.

"I still didn't like that fact that I had to lie to my parents. But I did. I told Bucky that something bad was going to happen to me for stealing and lying. He said if God didn't want us to have the money he'd have caused the safe not to open. And that was good enough for me.

"That week in school he bought me double lunches and ice cream. And after football practice we'd stop at the store and get whatever we wanted. His favorite band was Jethro Tull and he'd play Aqua Lung with the volume knob on ten with the windows down. The girls loved it, and he loved that the girls loved it. And I loved it too. It was a week for the history books. In fact, I kissed my ex-wife that week for the first time. Man she was a great kisser.

"That week in football we were playing Karns City. They were undefeated, and so were we. We had the biggest line in the league that year, on both offense and defense. On offense I played right tackle and Bucky played right guard, which meant we were right beside each other. He was a little quicker off the ball so the he got to play guard and pull around the end to block on sweeps and traps.

"It was a packed house on that hot Friday night. A-C Valley Falcons versus the Karns City Gremlins. Cars were parked a mile down to the old drive-in, both sides of the road."

"I remember that game," Duck said. "What a doozy."

"Yeah, Duck," Larry said, "What a doozy. It was the fourth quarter and we were down by four points with three minutes left. We were imposing our will on Old Mel Semanko's prized 52 Stack Monster Gremlin defense. Those guys were dragging ass and we had them whooped. We ran trap after trap after trap. We got down to the ten-yard line and they were sucking wind. We knew we had it. Coach Bevevino called a sweep to our side. I still know the name of the play—38 Slant Pitch Green. Son of a gun. The play required that I block down into the gap between me and Bucky and then Bucky would pull out to the right and lead the running back around the right side of the line. Well, it was all going well until Bucky opened his damn mouth.

"All night he'd be trash talking and jawing with Karns City's defensive tackle. He'd tell him stuff like 'your mama was good last night' and 'your girlfriend said you and me were similar—from the waste up.' I told him to knock it off but he wouldn't shut up.

"The center snapped the ball to the quarter back, who then pitched it to the running back. Like I said, Bucky was supposed to pull out around me to the right and lead the runner around the end. His blocking rule was to hit the first man he sees past the tight end, the guy beside me. Usually that's the linebacker scraping down the line to fill the hole because the defensive end would come across to get the runner and the full back would take him out. The tight end and I blocked down and Bucky pulled out behind me. Only this time the defensive end didn't follow the runner. He stunted inside, which meant that Bucky had to take him. Bucky wasn't expecting it.

"I tried to block down on the guy that Bucky was bad mouthing but he was too quick and got around me. That's what defensive tackles are taught to do. When the guy in front of them pulls out to go down the line they are supposed to follow him and break up the play. When I whiffed on him he just pushed me to the ground and ran after Bucky.

"Like I said, Bucky wasn't expecting that defensive end to be coming down the line. When Bucky finally looked up, that kid threw a forearm at his chin that would make Beelzebub proud. All I heard was Bucky screaming in pain.

"Just as the defensive end was laying down the forearm smack on Bucky, that guy he was trash talking hit him low from behind. Bucky's leg snapped like a pretzel. I heard it. It sounded like a shotgun went off. I never saw anyone in so much pain. Not even in the war. The Vietnam war, Duck."

Duck grinned and motioned for Larry to continue.

"I picked myself off the ground and turned around to see that it was Bucky laying there screaming in pain. That kid he was picking on walked past me and said 'payback is a bitch, son' and strolled back to his huddle. That bastard did it on purpose."

"Yeah," Paul said, "and he deserved it too."

Everyone looked at Paul.

"That sum-bitch was talking about my mama. Nobody does that and gets away with it."

"That guy was you, Paul?" Duck asked.

Paul shook his head in affirmation.

"Well, I'll be . . ." Bobby said. "How about a rematch!"

"What?" Larry said.

"Yeah. You and Paul go outside. Let's see if you can block him on his ass. Sort of payback for breaking Bucky's leg."

"No need for payback, Bobby." Larry said.

"Yeah," Paul said, "I've had my share of rough times to get paid back for that one."

"I bet you don't go into Big Buck's Tavern, do you Paul?" Bobby asked.

"I quit drinking a long time ago." Paul said.

"Larry, do you ever talk to Bucky?" Duck asked.

"I go up there for a sip now and then. We're still friends but you know how it is. Everybody gets their own life and there's not as much time for old friends."

June 17th, Thursday—Sill and Larry

Bobby didn't show up today. He was on a non-typical long haul to Charlotte, North Carolina. He was delivering steel coils to a roll forming plant and returning with PVC pipe. He announced it yesterday, as if the place would not be the same without his big mouth. It was just the opportunity Larry had been looking for.

Sill brought Larry's breakfast to him, just the way he liked it—two eggs over easy, toast with butter and two pieces of crispy bacon. She sat it down in front of him and he gave her a customary wink, only this time it was different. He gently put his large hand on hers and thanked her again. "Do you mind if we could talk later about the project?" He asked.

"Not at all, Larry." She whispered back.

He was working on a small improvement project at the back of the diner. Sill decided it was time for a new grease trap for the sink drain and Larry, although he was retired from his business, was the best at these things, and the most reliable to get the job done correctly. Sill, in fact, hired Larry to do most things around the diner.

The morning crew had its breakfast and arguments, and like clockwork they cleared out at 9:00 AM, except for Duck of course.

"Are you staying for lunch, Larry?" Duck asked.

"No. Sill has more work for me to do so I said I'd hang around and check it out."

"Oh," replied Duck, who got up to get a refill.

Larry walked all 400 pounds of himself into the kitchen where Sill and the girls were finishing pies and preparing the special of the day—hot meatloaf sandwich with mashed potatoes, gravy, corn and a drink. "Something sure smells good back here!" Larry announced.

"Hey, big Larr. How's it goin'?" Jill asked.

"Oh, pretty good. Trying to gain more weight." Larry responded, laughing.

"You look sexy just the way you are." Betsy added.

Larry's cheeks were blushing beneath the thick beard and mustache. He looked at Sill. "You ready to talk about that project now?"

"Sure," she said, "Let's go back to my office."

Sill's office was small and cozy, with everything having its place. She offered Larry a seat and closed the door.

"What's on your mind?" She said.

Larry put his head down and rubbed his hands together nervously. "Well . . . uh . . . I just don't know how to tell you this."

"Is something wrong?"

"Well . . . no."

"You didn't come back here to talk about the project, did you?" Sill said.

"No."

"Larry, I think I know what's up."

"You do?"

"Yes."

"Well, what do you think I'm trying to say?"

"You're trying to tell me that you like me."

Larry's eyes widened. A single bead of sweat rolled down his forehead and stopped at the end of his nose. He wiped it away. "How did you know?"

Sill rolled her chair closer to the desk and leaned in, whispering, "Honey, girls can sense these things."

June 18th, Friday—Pet Peeves, Validation, Birds and the 1972 Steelers

"Grump, stop chewing with your mouth open." Duck said.

"Shut up Duck," Grump replied, "Your false teeth click when you eat."

"Oh yes," said Ray, "the old pet peeves."

"I had a pet once," said Chuck, "but I shot him for pissing in the house."

"Like you care if something pisses in your house," Bobby said.

Chuck flipped him the bird. Bobby told Chuck he should clean the black soot from under his fingernails before flipping people off. "That's my pet peeve," Bobby exclaimed, "Dirt under the finger nails."

"Hey Bobby," Duck said, "You don't have any fingernails. You chewed them to the bone."

"Well, Mr. Duck, did you know that when you blow your nose it attracts Canadian geese?" Bobby laughed.

Duck dismissed Bobby's laughter with a wave of the hand.

"I hate it when people don't use their headlights in the fog," Larry said.

"I can't stand it when people don't use their turn signals." Bobby replied. "I'd like to run those bastards over."

"You know," said Ray, "I believe my biggest pet peeve is litter. That's ironic, actually, when you think about it. I live next to a pig sty—offense intended Chucky—and I can't stand to see litter strewn on the road. They need to make the prisoners pick it up."

Chuck was not embarrassed in the slightest. Pigs are happiest in the mud and accept that they belong there.

"I hate bitchy people, complainers, whiners," said Bobby.

"You must hate yourself then," added Duck.

"And I hate it when someone pulls out in front of me, goes really slow, then turns two hundred feet down the road." Bobby declared, looking at Duck, who was famous for such and act.

"I can't stand the insincerity of salesmen," Larry interjected. "They'll say anything to get your money, then after the sale you're just a piece of shit they scraped off their shoes."

"I can't stand people crunching ice or potato chips or anything crunchy." Grump said.

"How ironic, Grump, you don't like crunchy peanut butter either," Ray added.

They all laughed.

"Well," Grump responded, glaring at Ray, "I don't like long winded bastards who think they know everything and have to use big words to prove it."

"Indubitably," said Ray with a slight bow of the head.

"See!" said Grump.

"What are you guys blabbing about now?" asked Sill, poking her head from the kitchen.

"Pet peeves," Duck said.

"Oh. Let's see, I have one," she said. "I hate it when old men gather for an hour every morning at the same diner, eat the same food and get served without ever having to order, and NEVER tipping the cook!"

"Here!" Grump pulled a dollar from his pocket and slammed it onto the table. "Don't ever say I never gave you anything!"

"I've never said that, Grump. You've given me plenty of headaches."

Laughter erupted again.

"Yeah," said Grump, amid the laughter, "I've hear that more than my share of times from women. 'I've got a headache. I've got a headache.'"

"My old lady tells me she's got a headache and I just donkey punch her," Bobby said.

"What's a donkey punch?" Ray inquired.

"I jack her in the side of the head, knock her out, get on and ride and say 'yee-haw!'"

"I believe they make places for people like you," Ray said.

"Yeah." Bobby took a drag of his cigarette. "They're called whore houses!"

"You should suffer for such things," Ray concluded.

Ed spoke up, "My pet peeve is someone taking the Lord's name in vain."

"I thought you weren't offended by that," said Grump.

"I never said I wasn't offended."

"Yes you did."

"Listen, Grump, why don't you come to church with me and get some religion."

"Religion? I've had enough of that. Jesus Christ, I've had all the religion I can take. That damn Oral Roberts, what kind of name is Oral anyway? Sounds sexual."

"My preacher is very different, Grump. He doesn't ask for money like those TV preachers do. His name is Bates. Pastor Bates."

"Did you say 'Master Bates?'" Grump asked.

Laughter erupted.

Ed refused to react.

"I faced death a hundred times in the war," Grump continued, "and I fought hand to hand with the Germans and watched them die on the end of my bayonet, and the more I killed the more I wondered why a loving god would let this happen."

The diner fell silent. "Answer that one for me, preacher man."

Ed paused. "Grump, I was in the war too and I faced death, not as much as you, but I faced it. And I asked the same question. But the answer I came up with is that there is no answer, at least there's not one that I can understand. But that's where faith comes in. You've got to have the faith that God is love and you can have a personal relationship with Him."

Grump took a drink of coffee. "You can have your religion, Ed. It doesn't work for me."

"Well," Ed said, "I'm sorry to hear that."

"My pet peeve," Bobby said, "is listening to two old farts fight about religion."

"Not funny, Bobby, not funny." Duck said.

Validation

Duck got up to give everyone a refill. He accidentally spilled a drop of hot coffee on Grump's leg. "Watch what you're doing, Duck!"

"Sorry about that."

Grump's face was red as he grabbed a napkin and started to blot his pant leg, "Damn it, that hurt." He said. "Why the hell do you have to get up every five minutes to refill coffee? I didn't need a refill and you still poured it."

Duck put the coffee pot back and sat down without responding.

"Well," said Ray, "he has a need to be validated and accepted. In fact, all humans have a need to validate themselves. This is evident and proven through our actions toward one another."

"What the hell is he talkin' about now?" Bobby asked, as he took a drag on his cigarette. "That sum-bitch has an answer for everything."

Larry giggled, "Yeah, so do you."

"Well I ain't THAT bad."

"You ain't that GOOD either."

"Listen Larry, that old fart talks about shit nobody understands. At least I talk about stuff you can relate to."

Ray interrupted, "That's a fine example, gentlemen, of the need for us to validate ourselves through general conversation. In a discussion to get one's point of view across, the person listening to the other person's story is not really listening, but thinking of the next thing to say, like Bobby just did. The response is almost always in dispute of what the other person just said."

"Interesting," Ed said, "I do that."

"No you don't," Duck said, trying to be funny.

Ray was the only one laughing, "Very good, Duck."

"Hey Jim," Grump said, "before I forget, can I bring the Torino over? The damn carburetor choke is sticking again."

"Sure. I can look at it when we leave here."

"I can't. Have to go to the store then take the old lady to the doctor. How about tonight?"

"As long as it's before Johnny Carson," Jim said.

"You work that late?" Grump asked.

"Sometimes. I can't stand sitting around and I'm behind as it is."

"How about eight o'clock then?"

"That'll do."

Ray broke in on the murmuring, like he was quieting a class. He clapped his hands, "Hey! Here's the best part."

Duck got up to give refills and intentionally bypassed Grump.

"Give me a goddamn refill, Duck. And don't spill it this time."

"Nope. Get it yourself."

"Aw, are you gonna stay mad?"

"Nope. And I ain't refilling your coffee anymore either."

Ray was perturbed, "Stop fighting and listen! Now . . . it is totally natural for humans to validate themselves. Everyone wants to belong to something. Look at us. We come here every morning, eat the same thing for breakfast, and talk about nothing most of the time. But how many of you miss this when you can't make it? I know I do."

"Me too," Ed said.

Most of them shook their heads in agreement.

"See," Ray explained, "that's called exclusivity. Abraham Maslow, a prominent psychologist who died just a couple years ago, established what he termed the human Hierarchy of Needs. It was like a pyramid, with the highest needs on top and the lowest on the bottom. The lowest being food and water, basic physical needs, and the highest need was the need to belong. He called it Self Actualization."

"Don't you mean self masturbation?" Bobby exclaimed.

A few chuckles were heard. Ray acted like he didn't hear it, as did Ed.

"Belong to what, Ray?" Ed asked.

"To a group or club or something exclusive, like a family," Ray replied.

"Oh," Ed said. "That's understandable."

"Yeah," Grump said, "that's why people join religious cults. Like that church you go to Ed."

Ed looked down and rubbed his thumb on the handle of his coffee cup and didn't respond.

"Grump," Duck yelled, "why the hell do you have to be so rude to people?"

"Why the hell do you have to be so clumsy? And why do you have to be such a kiss-ass?"

"Are you crazy old farts fighting again?" Jill asked, coming from the kitchen.

"Yeah," Bobby said, "they're gonna take out their false teeth and gum each other to death."

They all laughed, except Grump.

"I'll have you know I can still whoop your trucker ass," Grump yelled, shaking his fist.

"Whoa, easy Grump. No need to get bent out of shape." Bobby said. "Besides, I don't want a reputation for kicking an old fart's ass."

"Screw you and the horse you rode in on," Grump replied.

Larry interjected, "I'll take the two of you outside and we'll settle this like men. Knock it off! Sill doesn't deserve this crap in her place of business."

"That's right," Duck added.

Sill heard the yelling and came out of the kitchen with a spatula, "Listen," she said, pointing at Grump, "you too," pointing at Bobby, "if the two of you can't act civil, one or both of you needs to go home and cool off. And if you keep fighting, I'll have Larry throw you out. Understood?"

"I have to go anyway," Bobby said as he rubbed out his cigarette in the ash tray, "I have to take my truck up to Hunters in Eau Claire and get the tires changed. See y'all later. See ya, Grump ass."

Grump didn't look at Bobby. He took a drink of coffee and looked at Ray, who continued his lecture.

"You see, gentlemen," Ray said, "despite the fact that two people are talking, it's really one-sided. There's no communication when it becomes a dual. My students used to say that my classes were one-sided because I was the only one talking. But that's not true. You don't have to talk to communicate."

Ed ate the last bite of his toast and washed it down with coffee. "Reminds me of church."

"Sort of like that," Ray said. "True communication is when someone is listening on purpose and the other is talking without the fear of being interrupted."

"Hey Ray!" Duck interrupted, "What did you say?" Laughter erupted.

"Pardon me," Ray said, "I got off track. Validation. Yes . . . well, I know that I seek validation through women. My mother coddled me, although I did not have a tremendous Oedipus complex, she provided validation that my father did not."

"Ed-a-puss. Yes, Ed is a puss!" Grump said, evoking laughter. Even Sill, although busy in the kitchen, was able to hear most of what went on in the dining area, like a mother with children who can watch TV, read a book, and know what the children are doing upstairs, all at the same time.

"Actually," Ray said, "Oedipus was a Shakespearean character who had a strong fetish for his mother."

"Fetish?" Jim said, "Is that like the cheese?"

They all chuckled again, even Ed.

"Fetish," Ray explained, "is an obsession, a fixation."

"I think I just lost my appetite," Duck said.

"Well," said Ray, "where was I? Oh yes, validation. You see, because my mother coddled me, I grew up seeking validation through women. I became quite a charmer, not because I was genuinely charming, but because I was driven by a desire for women to like me. And when they finally accepted me, through sex or strong emotional ties nonetheless, I moved on to the next one. It was a trap set by my inflated ego, you see. A never-ending cycle. And with each episode, my appetite for validation grew larger."

"What happens when they can't be charmed?" Jim asked.

"Excellent question." Ray replied.

During Ray's speech, Larry got up and went to the bathroom, then went into the kitchen to talk to Sill.

"What's he talking about now?" Sill asked.

"Charming a woman." Larry said.

"Well, if you ask me, that's pretty charming." Sill said with a big smile.

Larry smiled back and winked, "I don't know much about that."

"More than you realize," Sill said. "Hey, can you plunge the toilet for me. Betsy clogged it. I told her not to flush the tampons, but she won't listen."

"Sure," Larry said.

Ray answered Jim's question. "Well, I've only met a few ladies that couldn't be charmed. There are two reasons a woman can't be charmed. First of all, they were soured on men and vowed to never trust them again, or secondly, they were lesbian."

"You tried to charm a lesbian?" Jim said.

"Well, I didn't know she was a lesbian. And at the time she didn't either, I guess."

"I'm sure Bobby would have plenty to say about that if he were still here," Duck added.

"Let's get back to the subject." Ray said. "If I was unable to charm the girl, I'd go crazy trying. After some time, I'd feel like a failure. If there were one hundred women and I could charm ninety nine, I'd feel like a failure for not being able to charm that one. Eventually, I'd give up, tuck my tail and move on. Those were the ones that always left emotional scars."

"Okay," Ed said, "so let me ask you a question, Ray. How is it that you've been able to stay married so long to the same woman? It doesn't make sense."

"Another excellent question," Ray replied. "Well, when I met my wife, she was one of the women I was unable to charm."

"You married a lesbian?" Grump said.

Ray turned and pointed a finger, "Grump, that's not in the least bit funny."

"Leave Ray alone, Grump, he's telling a story." Duck said.

"Yeah, Grump, since when did you want Ray to shut up?" Ed added.

"Since he started to talk about lesbians." Grump replied.

"Let's continue in a mature manner, gentlemen, shall we?" Ray asked. "Anyway, I couldn't charm her. So at the point when I was ready to walk away, she did something amazing. Something no other woman had been smart enough to do."

"What was it?" Duck asked.

"Well," Ray said in a quiet tone, "she broke up with me."

"What?" Duck said. "Broke up with you?"

"Yes."

"Why?" Ed asked.

"Because she was smart," Ray replied.

"She got tired of him talking so much," Grump added.

"How did her breaking up with you help the situation?" Ed asked.

"Well, if you think about it," Ray explained, "during my efforts to charm her I was trying so hard, taking her flowers, buying her candy, writing love poems, she figured out that the only way to know if I was genuine or not was to break up with me. The genuineness of a man is tested through a broken heart. Like a sword by fire. The harder it's beaten, the stronger it becomes. She figured if she tore me apart, and my love for her was genuine, it would only make it stronger."

"That sounds like fuzzy logic," Grump said.

"Maybe, but she hooked me like a fish. The strength of a woman, I learned, lies in their ability to do irrational things and hide the fact that they know what they're doing."

Grump grunted in disbelief. "So what you are telling me is that my wife is smarter than me."

"Most are," Ray said.

"My wife is a slave driver that loves nothing more than to keep me on a leash," Grump explained. "She sits at home and does a little cleaning and cooking. I'm the one who pays the bills, balances the check book and takes care of intelligent matters. She doesn't"

"You're proving my point, Grump." Ray responded. "She's trained you like a dog and you don't even realize it. You're like Pavlov's dogs. She rings a bell and you salivate for a prize."

"She hasn't trained me. She doesn't know how to train anything. She sits at home, watches her soaps, goes to bingo and gossips on the phone." Grump said.

"What do you think would happen if you left her?" Ray asked.

"I'd never leave her." Grump responded.

"That's exactly what a good dog would say," Ray said. "Loyal and co-dependent. Really, Grump, what would she do if you left her?"

"Probably get another man."

"Exactly," Ray exclaimed. "You need her more than she needs you."

"Why?" Grump asked.

"Because she validates you. Somewhere in your childhood you were rejected by a woman and now you will do anything to keep one, including doing everything for her," Ray said.

Grump scratched his stubby cheek, "My mother was a drunk and wanted to give me up for adoption. My uncle took me in and raised me by himself. I don't even have a goddamn picture of her."

Ray retreated. "Grump, you fought for your country and because of you we are all free to come here every day and throw this stuff around."

"Yeah, Grump, you old fart," Duck said, "thanks."

Birds

"I hit a bird on the way here this morning," Grump said. "It stuck in my grill."

Duck looked out the window, "Boy, you got 'em good, Grump."

"Did I ever tell you guys my bird story?" Ray asked.

"No, but here's mine," Bobby said as he held his middle finger in the air.

Ray ignored Bobby and took a drink of coffee. "Well," Ray said, "I was just a youngster, maybe no more than ten or eleven, but I remember it like it was yesterday.

"My grandpappy had a lot of children and lived on a farm over in Perry Township. He raised beef cattle and took them to the Belknap auction every month. I used to go with him and chase the girls. My dad lost his job so we lived with my grandparents on the farm for a couple summers and dad helped out.

"Pappy loved to have family gatherings. And on one such occasion we were gathered around the picnic table eating. The kids ate fast so they could go play in the barn. Pappy tied a rope to the rafters above the hay and we'd swing way out and back. Sometimes we'd jump into the hay and get chaff in the nose. One time I jumped and disappeared. Pappy had to dig me out.

"I loved helping feed the cows too. I'd see the lights on in the barn in the evening and I'd run down to help. One time Pappy told me to put some hay down the feeding bin. It wouldn't go down so I jumped on it and down I went into the cow stall. The next thing I saw was a big black nose sniffing me. It snorted and blew snot all over my face. Those were wonderful times.

"Anyway, I got sidetracked there. Uh, oh yes, the picnic; I finished eating that day and instead of running to the barn, my cousin Jason and I ran out onto the porch to swing. I saw a bird's nest in the vines growing up the side of the porch post and wanted to see if there were any baby birds there. I climbed up and looked into the nest. No birds. But there were four light blue eggs. Robin eggs. Jason suggested that we take them over and show Pappy. So I grabbed them and took them over to the picnic table across the yard. I showed them to my mother and she went into a rage. She said that those little birds won't live now because the mother will smell my scent on them and abandon them. I started to cry.

"To make things worse, she cut a switch from the lilac bush and started to whip me with it. She made me walk across the yard and put the eggs back, and all the time she was whipping me. I never forgot that. Then at thirty years old I found out something that threw me for a loop.

"I was talking to a colleague of mine who was a biology professor. I told him this story and he said, 'Ray, I hate to tell you this, but, birds can't smell. They don't have olfactory lobes.'"

"What'd you do?" Duck asked.

"Well, the first thing I did was call my mother and told her that birds can't smell. Then I reminded her of what happened with the bird eggs. We had a good laugh over it. 'You still deserved it,' she said."

1972 Steelers

"Do you think the Steelers will do anything this year?" Duck asked anyone.

"Hell no," said Grump, "that damn Bradshaw ain't worth a lick."

"Yeah, they need to fire Chuck Noll. They'll never win the Super Bowl as long as he's the coach." Bobby added.

"Just wait a minute fellas," Larry said, "give it a chance. I hear Noll is pretty good. And Bradshaw has an arm like a canon. I heard he threw the javelin a hundred yards in college."

"I don't care how far he can throw a javelin or a football, can he throw on target?" Bobby asked.

"I think they'll do pretty good this year," Ed added. "They have Joe Greene on defense."

"I can see you know nothin' about football, Ed." Bobby declared.

"Well, let's see, Bobby." Ed replied. "They finished 6 and 8 last year. Bradshaw threw twenty-two interceptions and thirteen touchdown passes. And that was good enough to finish second in the division."

"So what's your point?" Bobby asked.

"My point is, Bobby, the rest of the teams in the division are really bad, like Cleveland, and we got the best running back in the draft—Franco Harris from Penn State."

"That kid is a rookie. He won't do anything for a few years." Bobby said.

Ed took a drink of coffee, "I bet you the Steelers win the Super Bowl within three years."

"You're crazy!" Bobby said. "I'll bet you anything on that."

"Anything?" Ed asked.

"Anything."

"Ok," Ed said, "If they win a Super Bowl within three years, you have to come to church with me one time."

"Ok. You're on. And if they don't win one, you have to wash my truck, right here, in front of everyone." Bobby added.

"Ok," Ed said, "you're on."

Bobby proudly took a drag on his cigarette, "Better start saying your prayers old man. I just got a free truck washing."

Larry chuckled. "I tell you what, Ed. If the Steelers win a Super Bowl, I'll come to church with you too, just to see Bobby squirm."

June 21ˢᵗ, Monday—Pappleberry Pie, Lord of the Rings and Heart Attack

Sill decided to try a new pie recipe and test it on the breakfast crew. Business was a little slow this month at the cafe, which is normal because it's the middle of summer and folks are on vacation or out early in the morning working before the heat of the afternoon. And furthermore, appetites wane in the summer. Winter and hunting season are the best times for cash flow. Sill was experimenting with peaches, apples and blueberries. After two weeks of trying she finally settled on a combination she could live with.

"If any of you guys want a free piece of pie, stick around for lunch." Sill said.

"I'm in," said Duck.

"You're always here for lunch, Duck," said Grump. He turned and looked at Sill, "What kind is it?"

"Well," she said, "it's Pappleberry."

"Pappleberry?"

"Yes, Pappleberry. Peaches, Apples and Blueberries."

"Sounds good," Larry said.

"Did you say we could have a free piece?" Chuck asked.

"Yes, Chucky, but you have to stick around for lunch. If you buy lunch I'll give you a free piece." Sill replied.

"That sounds interesting," Ed said, "can I get a piece to go?"

Sill gave him a funny look.

"I'll pay for it," he said.

"I don't want to sell it yet, Ed, because I'm not so sure it's my best effort."

"Well," said Ray, "why don't you let Grump have a taste, and if he likes it I'm sure we'll all like it."

"Grump won't eat it," Duck said. "He hates everything."

"Grump," Sill said, "come back here and I'll let you taste it."

Grump went back to the kitchen with Sill.

"Well I'll be damned," Bobby said, "Sill is going to give something away for free."

"She does it all the time, Bobby," Larry replied. "Look at how many meals she gave Tommy, God rest his soul."

"I kinda miss picking on that kid," Bobby said.

"Pappleberry," Ray exclaimed, "now that's bold. I once tried putting bananas, tomatoes and peanut butter on a sandwich."

"Yuck!" said Jim.

"It was awful," Ray said.

"Was it crunchy peanut butter?" Duck asked with a chuckle.

"Better not mention crunchy peanut butter. Here comes Grump." Ed said.

"What about crunchy peanut butter?" Grump asked as he sat down.

"Ray was telling us about a terrible sandwich he just made," Duck said.

"Well, Grump, how was the pie?" Ray asked.

"I'm not allowed to say." Grump smiled. A piece of blueberry skin was stuck to one of his front teeth.

Ray busted out laughing.

"What the hell are you laughing at?" Grump asked.

"Oh, nothing," said Ray.

Jim and Ed saw it and started to giggle, which progressed to uncontrollable laughter.

"What? What?" Grump said, his face turning red. "What?"

Ray walked over to Duck and whispered in his ear.

"Hey Grump," Duck said, "Look over here. Was that pie good?"

"I'm not allowed to tell."

Duck could see the blueberry skin when Grump was talking. He began to laugh so hard his upper dentures came loose and fell onto the table. Grump laughed, which exposed the blueberry skin most prominently.

Bobby and Larry saw Duck's false teeth fall onto the table and they began to laugh, then they saw the blueberry skin. Bobby nearly burnt himself with a cigarette, "Oh shit," he said laughing, "that's one of the funniest things I ever saw."

"Which one," asked Larry, laughing, "Duck or Grump?" His big belly was jiggling up and down and his eyes were watering. He could barely talk, "I think I'm gonna . . . uhhhhh . . . holy shit . . . I think I'm gonna piss myself."

Chuck was finishing his last bite of an omelet, "What the hell are you idiots laughing at?"

Bobby pointed to Grump, who was still laughing at Duck fumbling to get his upper dentures back into his mouth.

"Damn, I lost a tooth," Duck said, which invoked a new wave of laughter.

Sill, Betsy and Jill had come out of the kitchen to see what was up. They saw Duck holding his teeth and searching on the table for the tooth. Grump, still laughing at Duck, looked at Sill and said "Have you ever seen anything so damn funny?"

Sill saw the blueberry skin and put her hand over her mouth and started to laugh in a high pitch. At the same time Jill and Betsy saw it, began laughing and pointing at Grump. "Oh my god," Betsy said loudly. "Your front tooth is missing."

Duck was still looking, "I know, I know," he said.

"Not you, Duck." Said Ray, "Grump!"

Grump stopped laughing and felt his front teeth, "They're all there."

"Grump," Sill said, trying to regain composure, "you have a blueberry skin stuck on your front tooth. Looks like you are missing a tooth!"

Grump felt around and pulled it off. Duck was still looking for his tooth. He gave up and put his dentures back into his mouth. He looked up and flashed a big smile at everyone and started to laugh at himself.

"Hey Sill," Larry said, "Maybe you should call that pie Duckelberry!"

Laughter resurged.

"No," said Ray, "How about Grumpleberry!"

"That's the best laugh I've had in years," Sill said. "Free pie for everyone!"

Lord Of The Rings

Betsy could hardly contain her enthusiasm. As she poured everyone's coffee she flashed a dazzling diamond engagement ring.

"Who's the lucky fellow?" Duck asked.

"Jared," she giggled. "He asked me yesterday. He took me fishing and when he caught a fish he put the ring in its mouth and asked me to get the hook out. It was so romantic."

"Oh," Duck said, "well, that's nice."

"Say," said Ray, "speaking of rings. Has any of you gentlemen ever read J.R.R. Tolkien's 'Lord of the Rings?'"

"Can't say I'm much of a reader," Larry said.

"Well, it's terribly enlightening," Ray continued. "Tolkien was a professor in England back in the twenties. He had read everything under the sun. He was bored with the modern day writers, so he decided to write something he'd love to read. He'd get eighty thousand words into it and then scrap it and start over.

"Lord of the Rings is a tale of middle earth. That's the imaginary fantasy world he created. Anyway, in middle earth lived humans, elves, dwarfs and hobbits."

"Oh, yeah," Ed said. "I've heard of The Hobbit. Wasn't Tolkien friends with the Christian writer C. S. Lewis?"

"Yes, Ed. You'd be shocked to know that Lewis started out as a professing atheist, but I digress. Where was I?"

"Middle earth," Larry said.

"Thanks Larry. So, you have humans, elves, dwarfs and hobbits. They all lived in harmony. Until one day a schism happened that brought a split between good and evil. One of the humans went astray and made a deal with the devil. He'd overthrow the current rulers and take over middle earth. He did this by forging a ring from the bowels of a fiery mountain. When he wore the ring he'd be king. But it had a two-fold effect on him. As long as he wore the ring, all the good in his soul would be sucked from him and he'd end up pure evil and eventually die. It was a terrible price to pay for fleeting power. But it seems man is built to make these irrational decisions, which is what Tolkien was trying to say."

At this point Ray stood up to lecture.

"Middle earth split into two kingdoms, you see. One ruled by evil and the other by good. Eventually the evil overtook the good and it had to go underground, so to speak. This lasted for hundreds of years and the evil king finally died in a battle. The ring was lost and found several times over the next few hundred years, prompting the rise and fall of those who wore it. It finally got lost for so long people almost forgot about it, but middle earth would never return to what it was unless the ring was destroyed. And the only way it could be destroyed was to be melted in the same fires from which it came.

"Eventually it ended up in the hands of a hobbit, a wee person, a most unlikely of sorts to do such a dangerous task. Humans, elves and dwarfs banded together to help him in this task. Meanwhile, evil was doing all it could to prevent this from happening. An evil lord arose and literally manufactured evil soldiers, called Orks, and they set about trying to find the little hobbit with the ring and also waged war on all of middle earth.

"In the end, the ring was destroyed and middle earth was restored."

Ray sat down and took a drink of coffee. "That was fun."

Bobby lit a cigarette, "By golly, that was a good story Ray."

"You should get the book. It's better," Ray replied.

"I don't read much. Don't have the time. Besides, I'm sure they'll make a movie about it some day. They always do." Bobby said.

"Maybe. But books are always better than the movie. Just look at Casablanca and Gone With The Wind." Ray concluded.

"You're right," Ed said. I read both of those and the movies didn't do them justice.

Heart Attack

Ed grabbed his chest.

"Are you okay?" Jim asked.

Ed took a little brown container of tablets from his pocket and placed one under his tongue. He shook his head and his eyes grew large. He took a deep breath, "Wow. That was crazy."

"What happened?" Jim asked.

"Ever since my heart attack, I'll get moments where it flutters and I get short of breath. These are nitroglycerin tablets. Put one under the tongue and it shoots the system back into rhythm."

"That's weird," Bobby said.

"It might be weird," Ed replied, "but it works."

Sill walked out from the kitchen with tears in her eyes. "Listen guys, there's something I have to tell you. I just got a call. Paul had a heart attack last night and he didn't make it."

"Poor bastard," Bobby said.

"Everybody has to die some day," Ray said.

"Yes," Ed said, "but a heart attack is painful."

"Well," Grump said, "that's the way I want to go. It might be painful, but it's quick."

Epilogue

The Rose Buddies of 1972

1972 was the last summer The Rose Bud was open, and the last time all The Rose Buddies would see each other together at the same time.

Sill got sick with cancer that Fall and died the next spring.

Larry stayed by Sill's side to the end. He arranged for a hospital bed to be brought to his house so she could spend the last of her days in peace and as comfortable as possible. Nobody ever gets comfortable with cancer. They just try to manage it at tolerable levels. Larry held Sill's hand as she took her last breath. She had a big smile on her face. Tears were streaming down Larry's large cheeks and at the very end he whispered 'I love you' and squeezed her hand. One final squeeze from her and she was gone. He swore he'd never love another, and he didn't. He had taken off a hundred pounds during the ordeal. He put it back on in less than three months after Sill's death, and just kept going. Six hundred pounds was too much for his heart, which was broken, and now stressed from the weight, it gave out. He left all of his money to various charitable causes and took care of a few of those boys who worked for him and other whom he cherished in his life.

Ray had another dizzy spell, and this time it was serious. A stroke paralyzed his left side. He never fully recovered and died in the summer of 1973.

Ed's heart finally gave out for good one evening at the dinner table. He was having dinner with this wife and minding a cross-word puzzle. Ironically, the last word he filled in was *atheist*.

Duck was lost for a while. He finally found another café in Petrolia, just a couple miles from his home, but it was never the same. It was a winter morning and a fresh snow had fallen, dusting the roads and hiding the ice underneath. Duck decided to take a left and head towards Parker, in search of something, anything but what he had. It was like an invisible force was steering the car. He got to the bottom of Bear Creek Hill and lost control. A big oak tree took his life.

Grump and his wife were out visiting a relative and a thunderstorm arose. Lightening struck their house and burnt it to the ground. All of Grump's wartime medals and ribbons, along with his Army suit, perished in the fire. His heart was torn and he moved what little belongings he had into a mobile home. There he lived with his wife another ten years. He went into the bedroom one night and sat on the edge of the bed. He never set the clock anymore because there wasn't much to get up for. Just as he reached up to turn off the lamp a sharp pain tore through his chest. He was dead before he hit the floor. He got his wish.

Bobby drove truck and found another place to hang out and spew his mouth. He got into a fight with a trucker from Redlands, California and was stabbed three times in the gut. He survived.

Jim had aspirations of opening up The Rose Bud again, hoping to capture the same magic, but he could never pull enough money together to do it. Although he didn't know it at the time, he realized after Sill died that what they had there was special and relegated to memory forever. Never did such a hodge-podge of men come together in Parker, fight, argue, tell stories, and somehow get along well enough to want to come back day after day. Jim continued to work on cars, help out his neighbors, and fix the broken bikes that children would push into his garage. They called him 'Mr. Jim' and he delighted in helping them.

Chucky continued to pick up bottles and cans along the road for scrap money. Every morning he'd expect a rap on the side of the trailer to wake him, but none ever came. Ray was gone. The Rose Bud was gone. Tommy was gone. Larry left him all of his tools from the days of his home improvement business, hoping Chucky would do something more with his life. He sold them at a yard sale for a song; and went back to picking up bottles and cans.

Jill went off to college that fall. She went to Slippery Rock University and majored in business. She wants to open up a restaurant some day. It was all prepaid—by Big Larr.

Betsy finally married Jared. They had a fish shaped wedding cake. They had their first of ten children in 1974. Jared worked at the glass factory in Parker. Betsy stayed home with the kids. One of them came home one day on his bicycle. Betsy asked him how he could ride it with a broken chain. It wasn't broken anymore. Mr. Jim fixed it.

Photo Page

Pictured above is Cookie in the early 1970's. She owned The Rose Bud prior to Sylvia.

Above is the Allegheny River Valley looking north towards Foxburg, PA. The bridge at Parker is in the foreground.

This picture of The Parker House Hotel was taken in May 2007.